## About the Author

Addison Sparace is a young and talented author from Oneida, whose passion for writing has taken her on an exciting journey at just thirteen years old. She is a lover of literature and can often be found curled up with a good book. Addison's writing is infused with youthful energy and a genuine love for storytelling, showcasing her creative talents and her unique perspective on the world. When she's not writing, Addison enjoys time alone outdoors. Her work is sure to captivate readers of all ages and leave a lasting impression on the literary world.

Death and Deception

Addison Holli Sparace

---

Death and Deception

Vanguard Press

**VANGUARD PAPERBACK**

© Copyright 2024
**Addison Holli Sparace**

The right of Addison Holli Sparace to be identified as author of this work has been asserted by her in accordance with the Copyright, Designs and Patents Act 1988.

**All Rights Reserved**

No reproduction, copy or transmission of this publication may be made without written permission.
No paragraph of this publication may be reproduced, copied or transmitted save with the written permission of the publisher, or in accordance with the provisions of the Copyright Act 1956 (as amended).

Any person who commits any unauthorised act in relation to this publication may be liable to criminal prosecution and civil claims for damages.

A CIP catalogue record for this title is available from the British Library.

ISBN 978 1 83794 162 9

This is a work of fiction. Names, characters, businesses, places, events and incidents are either the product of the author's imagination or used in a fictitious manner. Any resemblance to actual persons, living or dead, or actual events is purely coincidental.

*Vanguard Press is an imprint of
Pegasus Elliot Mackenzie Publishers Ltd.*
www.pegasuspublishers.com

First Published in 2024

**Vanguard Press
Sheraton House  Castle Park
Cambridge  England**

Printed & Bound in Great Britain

To Megan Gillander, you got my journey started and I will forever be grateful

I would like to express my sincere gratitude to the following individuals for their unwavering support, encouragement, and guidance throughout the writing of this book: To my mom, dad, and stepdad, thank you for always believing in me and encouraging me to follow my dreams. Your love, and support have made all the difference in my life, and I am forever grateful. To Mrs. Bassin, my middle school English teacher, thank you for encouraging my love of writing and reading and for reading my books and giving feedback that helped me improve them. Your passion for literature and your commitment to your students have been a source of inspiration to me. To Gracie and Aeirelle, my dear friends, thank you for your unwavering support, encouragement, and enthusiasm for this project. Your feedback, insights and jokes throughout the writing process always helped me through my worst enemy—writer's block—and came up with interesting ideas to incorporate into the novel. To Matt Pelicano, who has helped me through my mission as a fellow author, and, despite our differences, his work is a great inspiration to me and I am grateful for the help I received from him. To Megan Gillander, the one who got me started on this mission. An ambitious woman, who has a heart of gold and helped me along my journey. She was kind and encouraging, even when times were looking rough. Thank you to all the other friends, family members, and teachers who have supported me along the way. Your encouragement and belief in me have meant the world to me.

# Preface

Six Years Earlier

My entire life has led up to this day. It's four in the morning and I lay in bed, fighting the jittery feeling in my stomach.

They'll be here any minute; I can feel it. I took a shaky breath and finally sat up. There was no use sitting around watching time slowly tick by. My stomach felt empty so I decided to go and get a snack. I threw my legs over the side of the bed and stood up. The house was dark and slightly cold. I was alone but that was okay.

I stood in my kitchen, slicing a variety of colorful fruits—kiwis, strawberries, and bananas—into a bowl. As I sat at my empty dining room table, my mind wandered to thoughts of my future. My mom was a nurse and my dad worked in a biology lab, so it seemed likely that I would follow in their footsteps. But they were gone now, along with anyone else who cared about me. I tried to push the sadness aside and focus on the present.

I carried my bowl of fruit to the sink, where it joined a stack of dirty plates and silverware. I returned to the living room and waited in silence for what felt like an eternity. Suddenly, a loud knock at the door jolted me awake. I stood up, groggy, and answered it.

A young man in all-black attire stood in the doorway, his pale face and black hair blending seamlessly with the early morning sky. On either side of him, burly guards with holstered guns flanked him. They were here for me, just like they had taken my parents and their parents before them.

"Hello, officer," I said, trying to keep my voice steady. Disrespect could get me in a lot of trouble.

"Good day, ma'am," he replied, his tone slightly bored. "Are you Maria Ann Denicdeivich?"

I nodded, knowing that lying would be futile. "Yes, I am."

He seemed surprised by my honesty. "Okay, I'll have to ask you to come with me then."

The guards moved their hands toward their guns as if they expected resistance. But, to everyone's surprise, including my own, I simply said, "I'll do it." And, with that, I turned the lamp off in my living room, stepped out the door, and locked it.

I held out both my wrists, expecting the guard to handcuff me.

He shook his head like he was confused.

"You don't need handcuffs. Just follow me."

I did what he told me to and followed him back to a sleek black car, only standing out by the shining of headlights.

The guards opened the car door for me and I got in.

The interior of the car was simple gray leather. There was a bowl of mints in the back as well.

They were obviously for the people they were taking away but I'd rather be safe than sorry.

I already know why these seats are black leather.

"Excuse me, sir," I say to the man behind the steering wheel.

He doesn't say anything but he looks at me in the rearview mirror, telling me to continue.

"May I please have a mint? I wouldn't want to have bad breath for the Queen."

The corners of his mouth twitched at a smile, or maybe a sneer.

"Yes, you may," he said.

"Thank you, sir," I replied and took a mint out of the bowl.

I was careful when I unwrapped the mint, taking the time to try and make as little noise as needed.

I successfully got it out and popped it into my mouth. We sat there in silence for what felt like an eternity but was, in reality, only a few minutes.

The vehicle slowed and we went through a huge metal gate. When we came fully to a stop, a completely different guard opened my door.

He saw my bare wrists and a hand slowly started moving towards his holstered pistol.

I panicked but the driver stepped out.

"She's good. Miss… Maria was cooperating perfectly."

"I understand that, sir. But she must have cuffs for the Queen's safety."

"It's okay," I blurted a bit too fast for my liking and held out my wrists.

The guard muttered something to himself and cuffed me. The handcuffs were tight and itching, and all of me wanted to scratch them off my wrists.

As I entered the castle, I was awestruck by the grandeur and beauty of the courtyard and interior. The oak trees, flowers, and lightning bugs added a touch of whimsy to the scene, while the white carpets and glass walls lent an air of elegance. I couldn't help but admire the paintings and plants that adorned the halls, feeling as though I had stepped into a fairy tale. When the guard led me into the throne room, I was struck by the sleek black throne and the rose vine that climbed up its back. The room was flooded with natural light from the glass walls, and the map table and bookshelves added a sense of purpose and intelligence to the space. I knew that I was about to meet the Queen, and I was quite nervous to see what she had in store for me.

I stood before the Queen, trying to stay as still and composed as possible as she circled around me, examining me carefully. A young girl, who looked as though she had been through a lot of trauma, watched us with disgust. Her blue eyes shone with distaste, and the bruises framing her collarbones made her look all the more menacing. I couldn't help but feel like one of us might not make it out of this room alive. The Queen, with her striking green eyes and prominent cheekbones, seemed to be considering me for some kind of test. I wasn't sure what it was, but I knew it was important. When she finally spoke, I jumped slightly at the sound of her voice.

"You'll do nicely," she said, before calling out that they were ready for the test. I couldn't help but wonder what my future would hold.

The guards at the door dragged a wooden table in and the Queen stood next to me with a clipboard.

She took off my cuffs and gave me a piece of paper. The girl had a chair too, and they gave her a piece of paper as well; the only difference was she was cuffed to the chair.

"We are testing your intelligence first," the Queen said as she gestured towards the table. I took a seat and accepted the pencil that was offered to me, noticing that the other girl at the table was doing the same. I tried to reassure myself that I could do this, despite the nerves that were starting to build in my stomach. "On your marks... get set... go!" the Queen called out, and the clock began to tick.

With a sense of urgency, I tackled the math problems first, racing against the clock to finish as many as possible. Some of the calculations were straightforward, while others gave me a bit of a struggle. As the science questions came up, I started to feel more and more out of my depth. I had no idea what gold's atomic mass was, or what carbon's atomic number was. Even defining an atom seemed like a challenge. But I did my best, determined to give it my all. Just as I was finishing up the first English question, the timer beeped to signal the end of the test. The Queen collected my paper and made notes on her clipboard, while the other girl's paper was ripped slightly as it was taken away. I saw a flash of anger in the girl's eyes, but she remained silent.

"Nursing abilities are next," the Queen declared as she placed a manikin in front of me and the other girl. "This man is dying. Perform CPR and turn the red light on the manikin's chest green within two minutes. Go!"

I hesitated for a moment, hovering my hands above the manikin's chest before finally pressing down twice. I knew I had to put my mouth on the manikins, but the thought made me feel uneasy. Despite my lack of experience, I did my best to follow the CPR steps that I had learned. The seconds ticked by, and I could feel the sweat starting to bead on my forehead. When the two minutes were up, the light on my manikin's chest remained red. My heart sank as the guards came to collect the manikin and the Queen made a note on her clipboard. I couldn't help but glance over at the other girl's manikin, where the light was a bright, reassuring green. I knew that my performance had not been up to par, and the thought of facing the Queen's disappointment made me break out in a cold sweat. I didn't want to die, but I knew that was a possibility if I failed this test

"Strength is next. Follow me," the Queen said, leading us out of the hidden door and into the courtyard. There, we found mats and weights waiting for us. "There are two parts to the strength test. First, see how many push-ups you can do in two minutes. Go!"

The girl and I both got down on the ground and assumed the push-up position. I closed my eyes and began to count, trying to ignore the burning sensation in my arms. Instead of focusing on the number of push-ups I was doing, I counted the seconds in my head, trying to gauge how much longer I had to go. Maybe all those years of playing Plieanth—a very hard contact sport involving bats—would finally pay off. As the seconds ticked by, I started to feel lightheaded, but I kept going, determined to do my best. When the timer beeped, I completed fifty push-ups.

"Impressive," the Queen said. "Get this girl a glass of water," she commanded, motioning towards me. A guard ran inside and returned with a glass cup filled with ice and water. I gratefully accepted it and drank it down in one long gulp, feeling the cool liquid wash away the sweat on my face. Wiping my head with the side of my arm, I listened as the Queen gave us our next task. "See how long you can hold the weight," she said.

I bent down and picked up the weight, noticing that the other girl was doing the same. As I paced back and forth, I could feel the weight straining my muscles, but it wasn't unbearable. It was like carrying goods from the market back to my house, nothing I couldn't do. After a while, the Queen grew impatient and called an end to the test at seven minutes. The other girl had set her weight down much earlier and was standing with her arms crossed, watching me with a mixture of resentment and envy. The blood on her face had dried, giving her a menacing appearance. I could almost hear the bitter thoughts running through her mind.

After a brief rest, the Queen spoke again. "I must say, I'm very impressed with you. Most people only make it to five push-ups at most. You made it to a whopping fifty. The longest anyone's ever held that weight was three minutes. You finished at seven." She turned to the other girl. "You held the weight for three minutes and managed twenty push-ups," she said, causing the girl to grumble. I felt as if the Queen was taking my side on everything, even if it didn't make sense.

"Thank you, Your Majesty. I try my hardest to please you," I told the Queen, hoping to convey that I was offering her a compliment. She seemed pleased with my words and actions, and I couldn't help but feel a sense of pride and accomplishment, but I stuffed those feelings deep down, guilty that I had them anyway. However, I knew that my fate was still uncertain, and the Queen had not yet revealed my score or whether I had passed her tests.

"Next up is endurance. The longest you may run is an hour. Your goal is eight miles. On this track, one and a half miles is roughly twenty-eight laps. Your time starts when you step onto the track."

I did a few stretches to ensure I wouldn't cramp up. The girl was watching me like a hawk and she copied me, doing toe touches, lunges, and arms swings.

I took some deep breaths.

Then I put my foot on the track. I started jogging to pace myself. I just remembered not to tire myself out. It shows weakness and I have one last test.

I made it to fifteen laps before I started to get tired. I couldn't walk, though. I had to push through.

I sprinted the last laps in an attempt to finish faster. It worked. I ran the last lap and plopped down to the ground.

"Wonderful job, my dear! I'm afraid I can't tell you what you got until later, but we have one last test for you! On to stealth." The other girl finished her run just three minutes before the hour was up. She was gasping for air and she couldn't breathe.

The Queen made a disapproving grunt, jotted something down, and walked us to the last course.

"The goal is to get to that manikin over there. Take the foam knife and stab it. But be wary. If you're caught by my guards, you're out. You can hide behind anything in the vicinity. Go!"

I ducked behind a white wall and scoped out the area. Two guards were patrolling one hiding spot, so I ran over to a different one. I was within twenty feet of the manikin. A guard was coming my way, so I rolled to a closer hide.

I was within five feet. I looked both ways and took out the foam dagger.

With a fast swoop, I came in and stabbed the makinkin. The other girl was already caught.

The timer beeps went off.

"You finished in record time, my dear. Let's head back inside." At this point, she was only talking to me.

My head was beaded with sweat, and I just wanted to sit but I followed her.

She retook her place on her throne and I stood in front of her.

"Are you ready to hear your marks?" she asked.

I wasn't but I said Yes anyway.

"Okay. Intelligence, sixty-seven."

I bit my lip.

"Nursing, zero."

I was sweating a lot.

"Strength, a solid eighty. Endurance, one hundred. Finally, a record, one hundred on stealth. Your final score is three hundred forty-seven."

I gave a big sigh of relief. But now, this other girl would determine my fate.

"You, Miss. Jenny, got sixty-eight in intelligence. A fifty-three in strength. Sixty-seven in endurance, fifty-eight in nursing, and a final score in the stealth of ten. Your final score is two hundred and fifty-nine points." She paused, then continued,

"I'm sorry, Jenny, but you didn't get at least a seventy-five in anything. So, you did not pass. You will be killed."

I almost pitied her as she gave quick frantic glances around the room. I could tell there was foul play; she should've scored more than that, especially on nursing when she was able to successfully save the manikin Quickly, Jenny made a bolt for the door. She'd barely made it five feet before a guard cut off her exit. I closed my eyes tightly and covered my ears. Then I heard the defining sound of a gunshot and a big thud.

"You, my dear, passed with flying colors. We'll escort you to your room. My stomach felt squeamish as I walked past her body, a hole in the center of her head, blood dripping out, pooling around her. I almost felt guilty taking my spot in the castle, but, in the back of my head, all I could hear was the tiny voice thanking god for letting it not be me.

They led me up a spiral staircase into a huge bedroom.

Light blue walls contrasted with lovely white accent colors. White draperies hung from several windows. A massive bed decked out with navy sheets sat on the wall you saw when you walked in. A wall-long bookcase was on the left side of the room and a comfy-looking armchair sat next to the books.

There was a desk on the other side of the room. There were a few paintings of landscapes as well.

The room was beautiful in every way. I walked in and stepped on the fluffy white rug in the center of the room. I looked around.

But something threw me off. In the corner, opposite the chair, was a weapon rack with all kinds of weapons, ranging from a 10mm pistol to daggers and swords.

And on the bed, laid out very neatly, was a black and navy blue leather bodice.

"You, my dear, are my new personal assassin. Based on my tests, this is the best position for you!" She sounded cheerful, which made me feel sick.

"A-assassin?" I stammered. "I will try my best. If you think I'd be a good assassin, I probably would be."

She smiled. "Trying is the most you can do at a new job. I'm usually not this nice, but you're different, Maria."

She was being unusually kind to me.

"Well, I best let you get settled in. At five o'clock the guards will take you back to your house to collect any goods you need. At seven o'clock is dinner, if you're hungry," she said, and left the room, leaving me alone with my thoughts.

I flopped down on the bed. The guards would take me back to my own house in just five minutes. I was tired, and mostly sick of putting on my fake "Your Highness" act.

The Queen seemed nice enough, but she was still The Queen. And she still had everyone take this unnecessary test. So what if it was her family's tradition? I'm pretty sure everybody, including the guards, knew this wasn't fair. Even she had to know it wasn't right.

Minutes ticked by like seconds and I heard a knock on the door.

"Come in," I called.

A guard dressed in royal blue attire came in.

He gave the tiniest, most spiteful bow I'd ever seen.

"Miss. Denicdeivich," he announced. "Your ride is outside waiting."

I paused. Why did he bow?

"Thank you, sir, and, please, call me Maria," I said, and politely asked, "Why did you bow?"

He gave a tight smile. "Because, Miss Deni-, Maria, assassins are the rarest, most valuable thing you can score. Therefore, you are treated better and guards are required to bow. Especially because you're the first assassin in years." He stopped and blinked. "Seven years, I believe."

I blinked a few times.

"Okay, thank you, sir. I'll be right out."

He smiled, and said, "Of course, Maria, and please no more sir. Call me Theo."

He gave a more graceful bow this time and then he left and closed the door behind him. And I swear I heard him whisper, "She's different," as he was walking out.

I glanced around the room one last time and headed outside.

Once I was in the vehicle, I felt weird.

I wondered what it was like for my parents when they got accepted. Did they get to gather their items, or is it just a one-time thing with me?

We arrived at my house in what felt like hours. I don't know why I was dreading it so much. I unlocked the door and stepped into my familiar living room. I knew there was nothing in there I wanted so I just headed straight to my bedroom to get a backpack. I threw in one decent dress, some sweatpants, tee shirts, and a couple of sweatshirts, followed by one pair of jeans. I put my toothbrush, hairbrush, and other hygiene items in. They were my more personal items. I put a framed photo of my mom and dad tucked nicely in a zipper. My tan stuffed teddy bear, my very first stuffed animal was going to be put in there but I decided I'd rather hold him. This small worn bear made me feel like a kid again, like my parents were here, holding me tight. I miss them so much. I was ready, everything I needed was in my tattered gray backpack.

    I walked back down the hall and to the door. In my head, I said I wouldn't look back, but, as the car sped away I couldn't help but look at my lonely house up on the hill.

# 1

## Current Time

I sat on the floor surrounded by my arsenal, methodically sharpening knives and cleaning pistols. It was a routine I had repeated countless times, day after day, with no other purpose to fill my time. Glancing at the clock, I saw it was almost dinner time, and I quickly pulled up my gray joggers and unzipped my hoodie to reveal a white tank top. I tied my hair back in a ponytail and made my way down the hall.

Strangely, this life wasn't as terrible as I initially thought. I had formed friendships with some of the guards, and the food was better than anything I could cook at home. Most importantly, I wasn't that poor girl who had died in a gruesome manner. I still remembered the sound of the gunshot and the body hitting the floor, haunting me like a curse. But, now, the sound of death had become a familiar background noise.

The Queen hadn't yet given me any extreme tasks, just small jobs, such as taking care of a merchant who had cheated her or capturing a person who had tried to escape their fate on their twentieth birthday. Over time, I had grown accustomed to these assignments, and, though it felt wrong to admit it, I didn't mind them anymore. Unfortunately, my past experiences had also made me suspicious of others, and I couldn't shake off the feeling that Queen Aria wasn't as good as she seemed. However, where I came from, the kind of scams that warranted punishment in this place were often overlooked.

As I checked the clock again, I made my way down spiral staircases and through winding corridors until I reached the dining hall. It was a magnificent room, with high ceilings adorned with blue paneling and gold trim, white marble floors, and dusty blue walls. A large chandelier hung over sixteen tables made of mahogany. I marveled at the grandeur of it all and then caught a whiff of the delicious smells wafting from the kitchen.

The aroma of warm apple pie, freshly baked bread, and roasted lamb with garlic and dill filled my nostrils, making my mouth water. Taking my seat at the same table I had sat at since the beginning, I occupied the chair closest to the door. Sitting at this table used to feel wrong, but now it was routine. However, I couldn't deny that I longed to leave this place.

The Queen came in and took her place at the chair on the opposite side of the table. So, we were looking right at each other.

"Maria, how are you today?" she said, with a smile.

"I'm good, how are you, Aria?"

I was the only one ever allowed to call the Queen by her first name, but we had an unusual bond. The Queen herself permitted me to call her by her first name.

Her smile fell a little. "We will talk about that over dinner, okay?"

That worried me a little but I agreed.

A short while later, people holding plates of potatoes, roasted lamb, veggies and freshly made bread came out. The chef rested a plate in front of me, the Queen, and a couple of other seats. I noticed one seat he put it at was usually empty. The food looked almost too good to touch.

The chef returned a second later with five glasses of red wine. One for me, the Queen, and the other chairs. We waited a little while for the rest of the Queen's council to arrive. Soon enough, a man and a woman strolled in and took a seat.

"Good evening, Your Mmajesty," they said.

"Good evening, Paul and Gina," she replied.

Gina looked around the room, her short black bob reflecting the light.

"Where is he? This is very important."

The Queen gave her a small glare. "He just got into town yesterday, give the man a break."

Gina just opened her mouth to reply, when a man dressed in a black suit came in.

"Ahhhh, Bennet, you're here," she said.

He took a seat.

"Let's eat, and I can explain everything to Maria," she said motioning to me.

He nodded.

The Queen took her first bite, which told us we could start.

I took my knife in my right hand and my fork in my left and started cutting my lamb. I took a bite and It was juicy and delightful, like always.

"So, what did you want to tell me?" I said, picking up my glass of wine and swirling it around in the crystal glass. I took a sip, feeling its cool, strong flavor in my mouth.

"I have your first real job, Maria. A man by the name of Koh Scott. He stole a fatal amount of money from our vault. Diamonds, rubies, and other precious gems too. Treason, you know. Kill him. And take back my money. And, as your reward, Maria, I will release you from your service. Four years early. This is a very hard task. We have no idea where to start. It may not even be possible."

She finished with a bite of lamb and waited for my answer.

I thought for a moment. I would love to get out early and start my life. I would kind of miss this place a little. But I would take the contract. Something seemed a little off with the deal; I didn't question it though. The last thing I wanted was for her to think I questioned her trust.

"I will do it," I said.

The Queen sipped her wine. "I knew you would. Bennet will explain everything," she said,

He looked slightly surprised but didn't disagree. He finished his bite of food and started talking.

"Kohl. He was one of the guards here. The Queen highly trusted him; he'd served for around ten years. He was her personal guard. But, one day, a large amount of money and gems disappeared. Over nine hundred thousand dollars worth. And so did Kohl. He took it, and now the Queen wants him dead. And her money back."

"I can do that,'" I said it with confidence but, in my head, I was second-guessing myself.

"Yes, you can," the Queen chimed in. "After dinner, one of the guards will come up and give you what you'll need."

I nodded and we finished our food. Maids came in and swept up our plates and the chef brought out plates with large amounts of apple pie and homemade vanilla ice cream. I ate it, but I could barely stomach it. I finished and headed back up to my room, walking through corridors that were dark, beside the few flickering lights of the nearby candles. I was almost on the spiral staircase when a hand touched my shoulder. I spun around, but no one was there. I must have imagined it. I kept walking, winding up the staircase and walking through more halls until I reached my room. I opened the door and the familiar place was somewhat comforting. I was super stressed; if I couldn't do this, would she kill me? I sighed, frustrated with myself. These were thoughts I had the first day I was here.

I heard the knock at the door and I stood up to answer.

Theo was standing there in his usual royal blue uniform. He bowed. "May I come in?" he asked. His voice had gotten deeper since I first saw him all those years ago. He was only a year older than me. He didn't even have a life ahead of him; he was stuck here forever. The guards didn't get a choice; they were born into it. If their mother or father was a guard, they were bound to be one starting at the able age of sixteen. They had to start so much earlier because it wasn't a very dangerous job.

"You may," I said. He smiled and walked in.

"The Queen has ordered me to bring you a few new weapons," he said. He handed me a rifle and some bullets and a small shank.

"Thanks, Theo."

"You're welcome, Maria. Be careful out there. I wish I could come with you. There's no adventure here."

I nodded. "Maybe you can come with me,'" I said.

He smiled once more, bowed, and left.

I lay on my bed and thought about all that was about to happen.

I even started to regret my decision.

# 2

I was way more stressed than I intended to be. Where did I start? I decided to brainstorm what I was to do. I sat up on my bed. Okay, so I was going to leave my phone here, in case I could be tracked. I decided to bring a handbag so I could easily bring my pistol and knife. It was a lovely red leather, with a tan fabric inside. Plenty of pockets. I put my weapons in one of the many hidden spaces. The next step was to make sure I looked casual. To make sure no one knew I worked for the Queen.

I looked through my drawers. Most of it was sweats and hoodies, but the majority of them all had the Royal Castle plastered somewhere on them. But I did have one thing I could wear. My mom's old cream cashmere sweater and a pair of black leggings. I walked over to my dresser drawer and opened it. I gingerly took the sweater in my hands and held it close. It still smelled like her. I decided that would be the outfit I wore.

I slipped off my sweatshirt and the cold air rushed at my back. I slid it on over my head. I took off the sweats I'd been wearing for over a week and put on my black leggings.

I looked at myself in the mirror. I actually looked decent. I grabbed the comb from my dresser and brushed my hair. It used to be shoulder length, but now the long black tangles were down to my mid-back. It took a while to brush out the knots, but it was finally back to its old straightness. I stared into the mirror longer, and my soft brown eyes stared back. I knew I wasn't ready, but I lied to myself and said I was.

I took one last glance around my now familiar room. A flood of memories that still haunted me came back. Even after six years.

The knock at my door.

The blood-curdling scream of the girl.

The fear I held in, because I told myself I couldn't be scared.

Even though I was petrified.

But I wouldn't let it hold me back. I threw a wadded-up ball of sweatpants and a tee shirt in a small drawstring bag.

I turned off the lights and, with a slow creak, I closed the door behind me. I started down the halls, for what may be the last time. My heart feels like it's beating in slow motion. I can't breathe.

I don't know why I feel so nervous. I've done this before. I don't know why I'm so skittish. Maybe it's because it's never been this important before. I finally make it down the spiral staircase. I rounded a corner and tThe Queen was there, waiting for me.

I jumped back a step, startled.

"Hello, Maria. I see that you're ready. I have pulled up Kohl's records. Seems he stole from some other people too, but that's not our problem. The escorts will take you up to the main city. That's where he was last seen. Questions?"

I nodded my head no, despite the number of questions flooding my head. My tongue was too tired to talk.

She patted my back. "Good luck."

She walked back into her quarters and the door shut behind her.

To my surprise, Theo was the one sitting in the driver's seat.

"Good evening," he said.

"Good evening," I replied. I was happy one of the only guards who was actually my friend was possibly driving me to my demise.

I sat in the car, fastened my seatbelt and the car's engine roared to life. We started moving, and I felt like I was leaving home all over again as I looked at the castle getting smaller and smaller behind me. The large stone and brick castle had been my home for six years, and the tall towers and rolling gardens had never felt so home-like.

We drove in silence for a while. The sky was black and the crescent moon was almost showing through the murky, gray clouds.

But, finally, he spoke. "The Queen said I could come along if you want me to."

I could tell he wanted me to say yes. If I am being honest, I'd rather do it myself. Alone.

But, looking into his sad blue eyes, I knew he was desperately wanting to go.

"Yeah, that's fine."

His face lit up and he just smiled.

We arrived shortly after our conversation.

It was dark out, and the sickly sweet night air stung my lungs as I got out of the car.

The night air smelled of rum. There must be a bar nearby, probably full of drunks.

Maybe Kohl was one of them.

Theo got out of the car, plodding behind me. Theo wasn't dressed in his guard's uniform. He was wearing a flannel button-up and jeans. His blonde hair was combed over nicely and his blue eyes were shining with excitement.

"Let's start with the bar," I suggested.

I saw his head move and I started walking.

"Wait!" he called.

I stopped.

" I can't see you," he said. I walked back over to his silhouette.

He moved his hand around by his side until he found my hand. He grabbed it and then said, "Okay, let's go."

"Okay," I replied.

I was glad that the black sky could hide my rosy cheeks.

With my free hand, I brushed my hair behind my ear.

As we walked through the dimly lit streets, the strong scent of alcohol led us to a nearby pub. We pushed open the heavy wooden door, revealing a room with oak floors and off-white walls. At first glance, the pub had a certain rustic charm, but, upon closer inspection, it was clear that the building had seen better days. The walls were stained with greenish gunk, and holes were prominently displayed throughout the establishment, giving it a questionable air of neglect. The sound of glasses clinking and voices murmuring filled the air, as a questionable-looking man served shots to the patrons sitting at the various tables scattered around the dusty floors.

As I made my way to the counter, a man with a bald head and a sleeve tattoo of a dragon greeted me. His voice was deep and rough, adding to the gritty atmosphere of the pub. I could feel his eyes sizing me up as I approached him, assessing me with suspicion.

"Whatcha gonna order?" he asked gruffly, his gaze lingering on me.

"Nothing, sir. I am looking for a man, Kohl was his name, I believe. Is he here by any chance?" I replied, trying to maintain a calm and composed demeanor despite the overwhelming sense of unease that enveloped me.

The man studied me for a moment before responding. "Last name?" he asked, polishing a wine glass.

"Johnson," I replied, watching his expression carefully for any hint of recognition.

"He's not here, but, for a bit of a price, I can tell you where he is," he offered, his eyes glinting with a hint of mischief.

I knew that this man was not to be trusted, and my instincts told me that he was trying to take advantage of my vulnerability.

"You think I'm an idiot, don't you?" I retorted, trying to catch him off guard.

"No, I don't. Why do you say that, ma'am?" he replied, his face reddening and his hand twitching.

I could tell that he was lying, and I wasn't about to let him get the better of me. "I know things," I said, leaning forward and placing my elbows on the counter. "Where is he?"

He cleared his throat, his eyes darting around the room nervously. "I said for a price I'd tell you."

"And what's the price? What's to say you aren't going to be an annoying little bastard, take my money, and then try to make a run for it?" I replied, making it clear that I wasn't about to be taken for a fool.

"You say try like it's a threat, girl. And, who's to say I'm not fooling you?" he shot back, his words laced with a hint of hostility.

"It is a threat. You don't know me," I replied, standing up and walking around the back of the counter, where cobwebs and dirt cluttered the floor.

Theo followed behind me.

The man stopped for a moment.

He pointed at Theo.

"You're familiar. But I can't quite place it."

Theo looked at me, silently asking if he could say he worked for the Queen. I nodded.

Theo came forward and stood next to me. "That's because I work for The Queen's Guard. I am this young girl's... servant," he said, almost forgetting no one could know my secret.

The man looked at his feet.

"Oh. I'm sorry Your, uh, Royal-ness. He's not here. But I-I do believe he's heading towards Stock, up by the lake on the northern side of the forest," he said, stuttering. I don't believe he was lying.

"I am going to take your word," I said. "But if you are lying, karma will surely come for you."

He nodded his head quickly, keeping eye contact with me. I nodded to the man and we started walking toward the exit.

We were almost outside when I saw the bartender in my peripheral vision glance at us, then usher someone into the back.

# 3

"Wait," I whispered into Theo's ear.

He stopped and looked at me.

"I saw him bring someone into a door in the back of the bar."

"That's sketchy," he agreed.

"Let's sneak around the back of the building," I suggested.

He nodded his head in agreement.

We tried to be as quiet as we could, but it was getting harder as the street lights were showing our shadows slithering across the walls.

We finally came across the metal door in the back of the building.

I could hear voices, the scratchy voice of the man, and a deep, rich, masculine voice.

Their voices were muffled but I was able to vaguely hear them.

"Kohl, a girl came here looking for you, do you know her?"

He thought for a minute. "Was it Carly?"

"No. She wouldn't tell me her name. But she had a queen's guard with her. The idiots thought they were fooling me with their servant bull-"

"Crap," Kohl said under his breath.

There was a short stretch of silence before the man asked, "What's wrong,?"

"Oh, nothing, John. I gotta go. Thanks, man."

The door handle moved.

I started to panic. What should I do?

I grabbed Theo by the shirt collar and jerked him behind a corner.

He glared at me, considering I almost choked him. I put a finger to his lips.

We were hidden behind a ledge and we watched as the door creaked open and Kohl looked both ways before exiting the bar. He started at a brisk pace, walking down the street away from town. Not even heading towards Stock. Theo and I started creeping slowly down the street after him, staying a good thirty paces behind him.

He went straight for a while but veered off into the woods on the back side of town. He glanced around, nearly catching us. He whipped out his phone and started aggressively typing a number into it. The phone rang for a minute before someone answered.

"Hey, man, we have got a bit of an issue. I think the old man's actions have finally caught up with him, but not in the way we expected."

There was muffled talking on the other end.

"Yeah, Charlie told me a girl came in with a guard and said they were looking for me."

More muffled talking.

"Yeah, I'll meet you up at the base in Charleston. See you there. Hopefully, we can get this all sorted out." He hung up, started to walk faster, and he ran into the brush.

"Looks like I know where we've gotta go," I said with a smile.

"Wha- no, you can't go there! It's too dangerous. There could be tons of men there that could overpower you- that could overpower me!" he said. He honestly seemed kinda worried. It was nice knowing someone had my back for a change.

"I know, Theo, but this is a chance. If we just stay quiet then they won't know we're there. We steal back the gems and bring them back. Then we, you know, find Kohl."

He considered it for a minute. "We don't even know that the gems are there, what if it's a trap, what if they see us?" he said with honest worry.

"That is a good point but they won't trust me." I grabbed his hand and yanked him into the woods, heading towards the distant hill in Charleston.

# 4

We trudged through the woods, the morning light bright on the horizon.

The golden light lit up the dark forest, casting shadows throughout the trees, making it look like imaginary monsters were crawling all around us.

We came into woods on the border of Charleston, the huge hill was closer and more visible in the background.

We walked onto the streets greeted by people walking about and the smells of freshly made cookies dancing around my face.

"Looks promising," I said to no one in particular.

Theo huffed in the back.

"Lighten up," I said, lightly punching his arm. "Worst things worst, we die!"

"Yay!" he said, the sarcasm heavy in his voice.

I grabbed his hand and pulled him forward. I could almost feel his urge to pull away, but he didn't.

We ran up to the hill, hiding in nearby shadows.

I saw several silhouettes on the hill, their dark clothes against the bright sky. I assumed they were my people. I crept up the hill, trying to be silent in broad daylight.

There was a small building on top of the hill. I wouldn't quite say it was a house though, more like some type of workshed. Big, muscly men were coming in and out of the shack, carrying big loads of timber, stone, and other construction materials.

We approached the shack slowly. A few of the men glanced at us, but none of them told us we couldn't be there. Until we tried to go inside.

There was a man who appeared as a sort of guard.

"Let me see your card," he said.

"Card?" I said.

"Yes, ma'am, I need your card or no entry."

Crap.

Did I need a card? Why did my only hope of freedom hate me?

I didn't have a card... but I had the fact I was here on official business.

Theo must have seen it in my eyes.

"Don't you dare," he whispered in my ear.

I ignored him. Partly because I knew he was right.

"I'm here on official business of Queen Aria. Let me through," I smiled at him, no warmth behind it, just pure annoyance.

I didn't even look at Theo, but I could feel him trying to keep calm.

"I'm her guard, sir." he said it too with a smile, but I could hear the strain in his voice.

The guard eyed me up and down.

I was sweating at this point. What if he asked me for my identification card? Not only does it have my age, date of birth, height and weight, and name, but it also has the role I play for the Queen.

"I guess I've seen you around town with the other guards, but I still need to see a form of identification. How do I know you're not a fugitive, and you and your little friend aren't trying to find a place to hide?"

No.

No.

Oh, no.

I can't show him my identification card. It says under my name, QUEEN'S ASSASSIN.

I can't have him knowing that. Especially because I don't know if he knows the target. Unless… I kill him. I've killed before. I don't know why this is so hard. There's barely anyone else around, just people working in the hills, and they can't see anything.

I glanced at Theo, just a split second I looked at him, and yet he knew what I was about to do. He gave me a nod and looked away.

"Okay," I said. I pulled out my wallet, the tan leather cool on my hands. I slowly unzipped it. I took out my card, the white plastic felt unusually warm. I handed it to the guard. And, just as he was reading, I pulled one of my ten-inch blades, the black rubber hilt comfortable in my grasp.

Some part of me wanted to know his reaction, but my more sensible half knew that if I waited too long, it would be ten times harder. And his last words are what helped me realize I made the right choice. His last words will haunt me forever.

# 5

"Don't hurt Kohl, don't hurt my brother." Those words, those were his last words. The last words before my knife came in contact with his throat. I wish I could say sorry. I wish that he could tell his brother he loved him one last time. I'm probably the most sympathetic assassin that's ever served. But, as I stared at his body on the ground, and watched the blood drip down his neck and start to pool around his body, I couldn't help but feel that, if I didn't do something, my prey would get away. And, as I took back my ID card, and took the ring of keys hanging off his belt, looking down at his body, he looked ever so familiar. The face of a friend that is just unrecognizable. I shook off the feeling that I had just made a huge mistake and I tried a few keys until one finally worked. I opened the door with a long creak. I didn't know what to expect here and, quite honestly, I didn't know how to kill this man. A man to me that is innocent but, to the Queen, needs to die. I would try to make it quick, as I always have, but I still feel like this is going to be different.

We stepped inside and it smells heavily of body odor, cheap beer, and bodily fluids. I don't even know what it is, all I know is that I already want out. There were stacks of timber, stone, cement, and barrels full of nails and screws.

I think it was some sort of storage shack. We looked around, and I had Theo lift some of the heavier piles of materials. The shack couldn't be that big. Maybe nine hundred or so square feet. But I had a feeling that this small building was hiding not-so-small secrets. We came upon a bookshelf with an array of books and, yet again, more building materials. So, of course, we did what any rational person would do. We double-checked that no one had come back yet, and started pulling all of the books off the shelf. And, of course, we were right, it was a classic; the ole bookshelf secret door.

The center bright red book, on the center shelf, surrounded by mostly mat books. It was so conspicuous that it stood out like a person wearing bright white at an all-black clothing event. But the secret room wasn't much to see. Gray cobblestone walls, dusty, cracked concrete floors. But there was a wooden desk and a bed with muted white sheets.

"I'm going to keep watch at the door," Theo said, leaning up against the open bookcase.

I nodded and walked into the dusty room.

I started by looking at the bed sheets, ripping them off, and throwing them on the floor. Nothing. I emptied out the nightstand, yet again, nothing but a few old sticks of gum and a pack of burnt-out cigarettes. So, I moved to the desk. The first thing I noticed was the piece of pristine white paper and a black pen. Among the pieces of paper was a half-written letter. I sat down on the chair and I swore that It would break under me.

I picked up the letter and started to read.

"Dear Charlie,

Thank you for your notice. I will head to Genoa Immediately. Twins have to have each other's backs, am I right? I will miss you, Charlie, and this may be my last letter for a while. Please pardon that, my hands have been fairly full lately.

Sincerely,

Kohl"

Before I had any time to even grab the letter, Theo ran into the room slamming the door behind us, then whispered into my ear, "They found his body."

# 6

Crap.

All of the books are still on the floor.

Shoe prints mixed with dirt and blood on the ground.

Soon after that blunder of information, there was a loud racket of a slamming door, and screaming men that were no longer censoring their language.

"Who murdered him? WHO DID IT?" someone yelled, their voice dark and gruff. We were dead.

"Barricade the door the best you can," I whispered to Theo.

While he worked on silently dragging the bed over, I looked for an escape.

There was a small window above the desk, I didn't even notice it before because it didn't even let any light in. I took a deep breath as I lifted the chair to throw it at the window. There was a loud shatter as shards of glass fell to the floor, giving me some cuts on my legs.

Oh, well.

I heard a bunch of deep, scratchy voices yelling at each other, "There, in the walls! How did they get in there?" Theo climbed out the window first, knocking the rest of the glass shards out. I grabbed the letter on the desk, then made a run for it just in time, and then the door to the secret room opened just in time for them to yell out an angry cry as we were running back into the forest.

I knew I shouldn't have looked behind me.

You never look back.

But I did, just in time to see one of the men half out the window; he had a bloodied nose. I turned my head back in front of me and continued running through the overgrown brush of the woods.

Theo and I slowed down just after we'd gotten deeper into the woods.

We sat in a shaded area, the sky shining brightly above. We'd have to get to a motel before dark; it wouldn't be safe here at night, with prowling packs of wolves and thieves looking for victims. I reached into my pack, grabbing a herbal salve and some bandages.

"You don't need to waste your aid on me. I'll be fine," he insisted.

"I'm going to patch it. Won't be much use with a half-rotted arm now, would you?" I said, giving him a half smile. "Take off your shirt," I commanded, looking away back at my supplies.

His face flushed a bright red. That probably caught him off guard, but, what can I say, can't fix a cut with the material of his shirt in the way.

He pulled off his shirt, revealing toned, muscular abs.

"Sit, it will be easier to patch," I told him.

He took a seat on the ground underneath a tree just as I warned him it may sting.

I put the salve over the cut and he winced. I wrapped the cut tight and fastened it.

"All good to go. Now, put your shirt back on," I laughed and smiled at him.

He gave me a cocky grin and lifted his shirt back over his head.

"Do you need any help?" he asked, looking at my battered cuts that were sure to leave a mark.

"No, thanks," I said, sitting down myself in order to spread the salve over my legs.

I will admit, it stung a little bit, but I didn't wince, I can never be weak again. And I never want to feel as weak and helpless as I did on that night, oh, so many years ago.

Once I was done and packed up, the sky was turning into a mixed palette of orange, yellow, and pink.

"We better get going," I said, "Don't want to be caught in these woods at night."

"Where to?" he asked.

"What's the closest town?" I reply.

"If I remember right, it's New Bay. Maybe not the cleanest town out there but it will work for a night," he said.

"Will do. As long as we get some rest. Lead the way, captain!" I laughed and saluted.

I'd never really known Theo, he was always just a guard, but he was actually a fun person to be around.

Meanwhile, I was brainstorming as we walked. Maybe it wasn't a good idea to just go for it, we already lost one life that could have been avoided. Maybe it would be better to befriend him, get him to trust us. Killing him may be harder that way, but it may be the best solution. While I was pretty sure that was the tactic I was going with, I didn't tell Theo. I had a feeling he wouldn't like that idea.

Just as the sun started to set, we made our way to the town of New Bay.

It was a small town with cobblestone streets and oil-lit lamps lining the roads. The town mostly consisted of little shops: bakeries, bookstores, flower shops, that sort of thing. But, after asking some locals, they pointed us to the way of Knotty Pine Inn. Theo swung open the wooden door to a rather vacant building. A stone fireplace lined the back wall surrounded by sheepskin furniture. The man at the counter looked rather happy when we walked in; I had a feeling they hadn't had any guests in a while.

"Hello!" he said in a cheerful tone. "Welcome to the Knotty Pine Inn. I'm Frank! How may I be of assistance?"

"Any open rooms?" I asked, making my way to the counter.

"Far too many, I'm afraid. What size room can I get you?"

"Anything works," I smiled.

I gave him his money as he handed me the key and he said, "My wife makes a lovely breakfast. It will be delivered to your room at eight a.m. tomorrow."

"Thank you, sir," I said wrapping up the conversation.

He gave me a nod as Theo and I walked up the stairs and down the hallway to our room. I unlocked the door and, I had to say, the room wasn't the worst. Pasty white walls, a small sofa, and oak hardwood floors. But there was one thing I had to complain about. There was only one bed.

"I'll sleep on the sofa," I announced plopping down on it.

That was a bad decision. The sofa was rock hard and I couldn't even lie down due to how short it was.

"I meant the floor," I said, sliding off the couch and onto the hardwood floor.

That, too, was a mistake. Not only was the floor uncomfortable, but it also was dirty. I had a feeling that this floor had never been cleaned before; I could see decades worth of dirt, grime, and dust.

"I-" I started before Theo cut me off.

"Just take the bed," he said to me, placing his bag on the sofa.

"No," I said stubbornly.

Theo sighed, running his hand down his face.

"Why not?"

"Because, if it's anything like that sofa, I'd rather just not sleep."

He sat down on the edge of the bed.

"It's not hard at all."

I eyed the bed and sat down. It was one of the most comfortable things I'd ever sat on. Not quite as comfortable as my bed, though.

"Oh," is all I said.

"I'll sleep on the sofa," he smiled at me.

Now I feel bad. Before I realized what I said, I blurted out, "We can just both sleep in bed!"

I was glad for the dim yellow lighting because, at that moment, my face was seemingly as bright as a tomato.

Theo also looked rather surprised, but he just said, "If you're okay with it." And that was that. I never wanted to mention it again.

I made my way over to the bathroom, putting on my pair of wrinkled white sweatpants. The bathroom was small and dark. It had white subway-tile floors, and patchy gray walls, with a small walk-in shower and the other amenities of a bathroom.

I exited the bathroom and threw my leggings into the bag. I sat on the edge of the bed, feeling a little awkward, when Theo sat on the other side of the bed and lay down. Soon after, I did the same. Laying down on the bed, I really hoped wasn't as gross as the floor was.

I had been laying there for a while, but I couldn't sleep. All I was doing was staring at the ceiling, into nothingness. I shifted a little in the bed.

Then, I heard Theo say in a whisper, "You can't sleep either?"

"No," I answered him.

He rolled over to face me. He looked tired; he had bags under his eyes.

He smiled. "Then do you just want to talk?" he asked.

"Why not?" I said.

We didn't have much to talk about, so I asked Theo a bit about himself. And, I'll admit, after listening to Theo tell me about himself, I felt as if I knew him better. He had three brothers and two sisters. Ben, Robby, Brenen, Rosie, and Carly. His father was the general of the guards. His mom made the best chicken pot pie. Theo has been a guard for about eleven years. He told me stories about when he was a kid and times he got hurt; he told me everything. I told him more about me, too. About my mother and father, about my life, how I moved here when I was six. After that chat, I was feeling tired. I closed my heavy eyes, and I heard Theo say something, but I couldn't really tell what he had said because I was drifting off to sleep.

# 7

I had a dream that was filled with such vivid detail and imagination that it felt like I was truly flying through the skies. In my dream, I was not a bird, but, rather, myself at eight years old—young, innocent, and naive. I was dressed in a polka-dot dress and my hair was short with bobby pins holding back my bangs. As I flew high above the clouds, I found myself soaring over the Queen's castle, seemingly flying towards my future fate.

The feeling of flying was incredible. The breeze through my hair and the airy sensation of soaring through the sky was unlike anything I had ever experienced before. But I didn't just fly around the castle—I flew all around the continent of Avion, experiencing all the different parts of the land. I felt the salty air on my face as I flew over the Cassandra Sea, smelled the rain as I flew through the Browen Rain Forest, and tasted the cool air as I glided through the snow-capped mountains of Mailen.

However, eventually, my flight came to an end. I started to fall, plummeting down to the ground with my stomach dropping to my toes. I couldn't even scream as I fell, and it felt like the fall would never end. But, then, someone glided in and rescued me, bringing me back up into the sky. It was Theo and, together, we finished our journey through the continent.

We flew over a small city that I couldn't quite identify, but it was stunning. In the middle of the city was a crystal blue lake, surrounded by a small town with bungalows and shops. The bungalows looked like those you might see at an ocean resort, with wooden exteriors and straw-like roofs. Eventually, we landed back at the place where our journey had begun: the Queen's castle.

The Queen's castle seemed to be a place where everyone was destined to go, no matter the outcome. It had a mysterious and almost ominous quality to it, as if it held some sort of power or significance. I was suddenly awakened by a knock at the door, still feeling groggy and disoriented as I lay in bed under the blankets. Theo was already up and moving, quickly unlocking and opening the door to reveal the inn owner holding a silver tray filled with an assortment of breakfast items. On the tray were eggs, bacon, sausage, orange juice, fresh bread and butter, hash browns, and a few other foods that looked less appetizing.

"Thank you!" Theo exclaimed in an overly cheerful voice, reaching out to take the tray from the inn owner. In a slightly rude gesture, he immediately closed the door as the owner was saying, "You're welcome," leaving him standing in the hallway. Theo carried the tray over to the bed and began portioning out the food onto the two plain white plates that had been provided for us. He gave me a slightly larger serving of the strange, orangish-yellow goop, but I didn't really want to know what it was made of.

I sat up in bed and thanked Theo for the breakfast, feeling hungry and ready to dig in. As I took my first bite of the eggs, I was pleasantly surprised by their light, buttery flavor, and perfectly cooked texture. The bacon and sausage were juicy and flavorful, and the toast tasted just like the kind my grandmother used to make—with the perfect amount of crunch and butter. Even the strange orangish-yellow goop turned out to be surprisingly good, with a warm, homey flavor that was almost apple-like. The orange juice was also delicious, with a fresh, citrusy taste that suggested it had been recently squeezed. Overall, it was a ten out of ten meal, and I couldn't help but express my admiration to Theo.

"This is amazing," I said, taking a large sip of orange juice.

"I agree," Theo replied through a mouthful of eggs. When we were finished eating, we left our empty plates on the bed that we had made, and I quickly threw on my leggings before grabbing our bags and heading out the door. "We should give them an extra tip for the food," Theo suggested as we left the room.

""Agreed," I replied, pulling out six chronos—the currency used in our continent, as other parts of the world had adopted more practical forms of money.

As we made our way down to the lobby, we saw a woman sitting in one of the chairs, her frilly blonde hair styled in an elaborate updo and her petite frame draped in a blue floral apron. She appeared to be crocheting something, possibly a scarf, with a look of focused concentration on her face. It seemed likely that she was an employee at the inn, perhaps working as a receptionist or host. With our bags in hand, Theo and I approached the front desk to check out and leave our generous tip for the delicious breakfast we had just enjoyed.

I walked to the counter where the too-happy innkeeper was standing.

"Thank you, sir. Have a wonderful day," I said, dropping chronos on his desk.

He looked shocked.

"Oh, ma'am. I-I can't accept this! You have already paid, and this….. This is far too much money!" he exclaimed.

"Keep it," I reassured him. "I have far more than that."

He shook his head in disbelief but didn't say anything more. The frilly-haired woman came over.

"Oh, dear, is this for us? Thank you so much. This will keep us stable for a good long while. Bless your hearts," she smiled, pulling me into a hug. She smelled strongly of perfume.

"Come back anytime, free room on the house."

I gave him a nod but I don't think I'd ever return.

We exited the building and took a left down the road.

"So, where exactly are we going now?" Theo asked.

"Genoa," I said with a cocky smile.

"When did you find this out?" he asked.

I reached into my handbag and pulled out the now wrinkled letter, and handed it to Theo.

He read it over, once, twice before handing it back to me.

"Okay, so that was his brother we... killed."

"Yes," I reply, not letting that comment dampen my stride.

We walked in silence after that.

It would be about half a morning's walk to get from the outskirts of New Bay to Genoa. But it would be worth it if I found my target. A step closer to freedom.

I continued brainstorming my plan in my head. I was still unsure if I would voice it to Theo; he may not agree and try to stop me. So, the plan was going to be as follows: First, I'd try to befriend Kohl. Once we were acquainted enough, we would become closer "friends". Then, maybe invite him over to lunch. And slip some poison into his drink. Perfect. Simple and relatively painless.

I continued that thought in my head as we continued walking. Only about another few hours and soon we'd arrive, at about a midday. I hummed a melody my mom always used to sing to me. It was soft and slow. It made me feel warm and always brought a smile to my face. I couldn't quite explain the sound, but it was some kind of mix between Sweet Caroline and You Are My Sunshine. I, to be honest, didn't even know the song. I just knew the way my mom used to hypnotically hum it, to calm me down in all of my anxiety-filled moments. And, at that moment, all of the dread and tiredness just washed away. I made sure to take in all of the scenery of the lush, green forest we were in. I kept that melody playing in my head and, before I knew it, I saw the sprawling cityscape in front of me. Tall buildings unlike any I've ever seen before. Black concrete roads. Cement sidewalks. Hundreds of thousands of people. Hundreds of thousands of options. We would have to find more than one person that matched our given description. It would be weird if we didn't. But that one word continued to replay over and over again in my mind: freedom, freedom, freedom. It echoed with empty promises, promises that I would never have back. Those promises were empty because I was making them to myself. But I didn't focus on that part, merely the part that I could be free, free from the shackles that have held me back all my life. And that, just that, was enough to keep me going. After that, my stride was taller and higher. I hoped I looked as confident as I felt.

"Where do we even start?" I started to sigh as we'd been walking for at least an hour. The hustle and bustle of the city was no joke. The sleek vehicles of varying colors sped by; blues, grays, blacks, and whites were the most common colors. The tall buildings stretched above the streets, towering above us. But there were also calm places. Smaller, less busy, roads with small brick buildings and shops. Walking through the city was like walking through a hundred different places.

"I don't know," Theo replied to my question. He grabbed the paper that had the description of Khol. He read the traits Khol possessed, including eye color, skin color, and hair color. Any physical things too: height, weight.

The gears in my head were failing to work, but I could see Theo's spinning at full speed. That's when I swear I saw the lightbulb appear over Theo's head.

"I think I got it."

# 8

"Really?" I said, not meaning to sound surprised but I couldn't help it.

"Let's go get some lunch, then I'll tell you."

I sighed but didn't argue because I was exhausted.

We walked to the nearest café, labeled Soup N' Stuff.

We walked into the café, relieved to feel the cool air and escape from the warm weather. We took a seat at one of the tables for two. A waitress, dressed in a yellow plaid dress and white sneakers came up to us, and, in what I assumed was her "I'm supposed to be happy at work" voice, she said, "Hello! Welcome to Soup N' Stuff. What can I get you to drink?"

"I'll have ice water, please," I answered with a smile.

"Of course, and for you, sir?" she said, turning to Theo.

"Coca-Cola, please."

She made a half smile, then started to the counter.

I gazed out the window at the busy street full of pedestrians and zooming cars. Genoa was a lively town with many shops and the streets had a good amount of color. All of the restaurants and shops had colorful signs, and even the tall buildings seemed to come in different shades of blue, red, and gray. It did have a bit of a stench, though. Not terrible compared to some other cities, but there were undertones of hot garbage and body odor.

She came back and handed us our drinks, and got ready to take our order. I hadn't paid any prior attention to the menu, so I quickly scanned it. Soup, sandwiches, noodles. That was about all they had.

"Can I have the metsubu noodles?" I asked.

"Of course. And for you?" she asked Theo.

"I'll take the chicken turkey ranch sandwich."

"Always a good choice. It will be right out"

Once she was gone, I stared at Theo.

"I'm waiting," I said. I didn't mean to sound snarky, but I was tired and hungry, and I just wanted to get it over with. The word freedom never ceases to play over and over in my head. I have to listen to it all day, the background noise to all my other thoughts.

"Jeez, okay, I'm going, well, this city is big, am I right? Big means security cameras. If we can find a way to hack into the city's cameras, if he's here, he's bound to be on one of them. Then we at least know the area to look in."

I thought about that for a minute.

"Yeah, that's a good idea."

He just smiled; he looked a little annoyed.

"Where do we start?" I asked as our waitress brought over our food.

The noodles I ordered looked delicious. These noodles were a bit like ramen, the same kind as noodles with chicken broth. It had chives, a fried egg, chicken, and hot sauce. I broke the yolk on the egg and stirred it in with the noodles. I twirled the fork around the noodles and took a bite. The warm delicious flavors swarmed my mouth, and it reminded me of my mother and her homemade metsubu noodles.

"I'd think the city hall would be a good place to start," Theo said in between bites of his sandwich.

I took a bite of my food. I didn't want to sound like a downer, but it was a long shot. Going back to my earlier thoughts, there is very little chance that it would work. Thousands of people, not all of them look different.

"Can I see the description paper?" I asked.

I looked over all of the attributes he had.

"Might as well start," I sighed.

"Oh, come on. Try to look on the bright side. You get to leave. You're one of the lucky people, Maria. People like me are stuck here forever."

Theo was right. I shouldn't be so negative about it. I am one of the lucky ones.

"Yeah, you're right," I mumbled. "Let's go."

We left our money on the table and got up to leave, but something caught my eye.

A man, with tall, dusty brown hair. I glanced at my sheet. It matched perfectly but I only saw his back.

"Theo," I whispered into his ear. "The guy in front of us looks like a match." My heart was pounding hard in my chest. Theo knew what he had to do, even without saying anything. Theo pushed back, dissolving into the crowd, it was better for him not to be seen.

I started walking faster, adrenaline pumping through my veins. I finally caught up, and I started to count my steps. I finally approached him, and he noticed me before I even said anything. I pretended not to notice as he studied me up and down.

"Maria?" he said, his voice deep and rich.

"Do I know you?" I said, turning around and looking into his ice-blue eyes. We walked off to the side of a building, moving out of other's ways.

"It's me, Khol," he said, smiling at me, showing his perfect teeth.

I know, I said in my head, but I replied with, "I'm sorry, it doesn't ring a bell."

"Khol Scott," he said hopefully.

Wait. Kohl Scott? That name rang a bell, but from where? Then it clicked in my head and I didn't know how I could forget.

Kohl Scott was my best friend.

# 9

First grade. Kohl was the first person to accept me as the new girl. We became best friends, sharing secrets, adventures, everything. But that all changed when he moved sophomore year of high school.

"Khol Scott," I smiled and laughed as memories flooded my head. The time we pranked Mrs. Johnson in third grade. Comforting each other at our hardest times. Suddenly, my heart started to ache. This was going to be a lot harder than I intended it to be.

He leaned in and hugged me, and the moment I smelt that familiar scent, I was flooded with nostalgia. That was the scent of cologne I got him in our freshman year.

"You still use that cologne?" I asked.

"I never forgot about you, you know. I was so angry at my dad, I tried to run away. I wanted to stay here, but we had to go where the money was, according to him."

I nodded my head. And what I was about to say was going to kill me. "So, how's... Has Charlie been? Same old sarcasm?"

Kohl's face dropped with sorrow. "I recently got a letter saying he was deceased."

"Oh, my god, I'm so sorry." It was heart-shatteringly hard to lie to the person that I had cherished for so many years of my childhood.

"It was so great to see you!" I breathed, trying to come up with ideas while also making sure I didn't lose him.

"You too! Do you live around here?" he asked.

"No, I am looking for a spot," I lied.

"You're always welcome to stay at my apartment, until you find your own, of course."

"Oh, thank you. But I have another person that I'm traveling with... would it be okay if they came too?" I held my breath, waiting for his reply.

He grinned at me, "Of course! I don't mind at all. It's Travis Corner Townhouse Apartments on Brown Boulevard. Apartment 396." He glanced at the silvery gray watch on his wrist. "Well, I've got to get going! I'll see you later." He disappeared into the crowd of people, my opportunity slipping away.

Theo appeared from the shadows, face stern, yet emotionless.

"Maria." He reached up and rubbed his temples. His fists were clenched. "What did you do?"

"I-" He didn't let me continue.

"That was your chance, Maria!" he roared. People were turning their heads at us.

"Please, Theo, let me explain," I begged. I didn't know how to feel or what to say. I'd never seen him act like this.

"I'm not sure if I want to hear it," he said, pacing the sidewalk. He was fuming.

"Well, you don't have a choice," I said, starting to get angry myself. I could tell this would be a heated argument.

Before he had a chance to say anything, I said, "I have had a plan all along. I didn't tell you because I knew you'd react like a total jerk. Just like how you're reacting now. But I planned to befriend him, then kill him in his sleep." I said the last part a little more softly. I gave him half a moment to let that sink in before I continued, "But things didn't go as planned." I was cut off by Theo who'd muttered, "clearly" under his breath. I glared at him, but the glare I got back could kill. I kept going. "But things didn't go as planned because I found out… I found out he's my best friend from, what, fifteen years ago? Oh, and to top that off, now I have to kill him, the only person who ever, and I mean ever, treated me like a real person. Listened to me, didn't get all fired up over mistakes, and was there for me when I needed him most. So, pardon me for acting out. But I think you're just being a complete brute, Theo," I ended in a big huff, my face red and hot. There may have even been some tears.

"That was fifteen years ago!" he shouted at me. "Fifteen. Get this number in your head! He doesn't look the same, won't act the same, you barely know who he is now."

"WHY DO YOU EVEN CARE SO MUCH!" I cried, "It's not even your life. It's mine."

"BECAUSE I CARE ABOUT YOU!" he screamed. That made me pause and, yet again, several heads turned. Some people even stopped and watched, but Theo scowled at them until they left. "I don't want you to die, because you didn't complete a task I know you can do. No matter what you say, I have tried my best to treat you like a real person, because you're one of the first people who's treated me like- like someone alive, here. Not some servant to be ordered around and treated like a toy." He looked at the ground and held his arms.

So, I would die if I couldn't do it? I sighed. "I think we both need time away from each other," I told him, handing him the piece of paper where Kohl's address was scribbled down. I didn't even wait for his reply before I stomped off down the street.

# 10

Kohl's apartment complex was nice for being in one of the crappier parts of Genoa. It was a row of brick townhouses, with freshly cut lawns, and pretty flower gardens. In the strip of land between the sidewalk and the lawns, there was a large metal plaque labeled, Travis Corner Townhouse Apartments. I walked up to his door; it was bright red. I knocked on the door three times and stood there waiting for a reply. A few seconds later, the door creaked open to reveal Kohl standing there.

"Nice to see you again, stranger. Come on in," he announced, opening the door wider, beckoning me to come inside.

The inside of his townhouse was small and cramped, yet it had a homey feel. As soon as you stepped inside, you were greeted by a foyer, with a small, narrow wooden staircase. Then, there was a hallway leading back into the rest of the house. The natural mahogany floors gave an older feel to the house but in a good way. The walls were muted tan. We walked into a living room with brown leather furniture and a small TV.

"Where is your other friend?" he asked.

"We had a bit of a falling out. He'll come around sometime and, if he doesn't, fine by me."

Khol just nodded.

"Make yourself at home," he said, then left for the kitchen.

I followed him. "Do you mind if I take a shower? I haven't had one of those in a day or two."

"No need to ask," he replied, then added, "Let me show you to the bathroom."

We walked back to the stairs and headed up them, leading to a hallway with three doors. He opened the door on the left. It was a smaller bathroom, with white tile floors, dim yellow lighting, and a shower tub with an old floral shower curtain.

"Would you like me to wash your clothes?" he asked.

"I wish I could, but I have nothing to change into."

"I'll be right back," he said and walked into the room across the hall.

He came out with a pair of gray sweatpants and a tee shirt.

"Here, wear these. We can wash your clothes in the meantime."

"Thank you," I said and, once he'd gone downstairs, I closed the door behind me.

I stripped out of my grime-covered clothes and dropped them on the floor. I placed Kohl's clothes on the sink and examined my bare body in the mirror. We'd only traveled about a week, but my body was battered. Bruises and scrapes that still didn't heal. You could see some of my ribs. I grabbed a comb that sat on the sink and started prying at my knotted hair, trying to untangle it to the best of my ability. Once it was relatively smooth, I started the water, making it as hot as it could go. A part of me felt like, if the water was hot enough, it may melt all of my problems away. Once the shower was steamy, I grabbed a loofah and stepped inside. I arched my back when my skin first hit the water, not expecting it to be as hot as it was. But I liked the feeling of the hot water pouring down my back. It was rather comforting. I started by squeezing the shampoo onto my scalp and scrubbing until I wasn't sure I even had one left. I added in the conditioner, then started aggressively washing my body, my legs, arms, torso, and chest, nothing could escape the wrath of me with a fresh loofah. Then I just stood there under the boiling water, letting my worries melt away, hoping they'd go down the drain. I shut the water off and toweled my body and my hair dry. I put my undergarments back on, then I put on the sweatpants. They were five sizes too big, and I had to pull the string snugly around my small waist. The shirt was also huge, but it looked comfortable. I slipped it over my head and balled up my clothes in my towel. I opened the door and was greeted by a blast of cold. I guess I hadn't realized how hot it was in there.

    I walked down the stairs and found Kohl reading a book on the sofa. How could such an innocent boy be a criminal? I let myself ponder that thought as I handed him the ball of clothes. He opened up a door that revealed a little washer and dryer. He threw them in with some detergent and then started it.

"Are you hungry?" he asked. I never finished my noodles, but I just said, "No, thank you though." I didn't want to be a burden.

"Food is in the fridge if you change your mind."

Then I heard a knock on the door. Both Kohl and I got up and walked to the door, and I stood back when he answered it.

It was Theo.

"Can I help you?" he asked.

"That's my friend," I informed him.

"Oh, come on in! I'm Kohl. Nice to meet you."

Theo just nodded and Kohl seemed to understand he was still angry at me. Theo came inside, taking his shoes off at the door.

"Your house is lovely," Theo said.

"Thank you," Kohl replied.

Theo took a deep breath and closed his eyes. "I apologize for being rude. I'm so tired. My name is Theo." He held out his hand and shook Kohls.

"It's quite okay. We all have those days, I understand. Feel free to make yourself at home. A friend of Maria's is a friend of mine." Kohl then turned to me and said, "Are you going to want to stay here tonight?"

Ignoring Theo's silent protest telling me to say no, I said, "Yes, please."

He walked us up to the guest room, set up with a twin-sized bed and a sofa.

"It's not much, but better than the streets, am I right?"

"Yes. Thank you so much but, if you'll excuse us, I need to have a chat with Maria," Theo said, in what I bet he thought was his most polite voice.

"Of course," he said, leaving the room and shutting the door behind him.

"What is it now?" I asked.

"Are you crazy? What if he knows it's you? What if he tries to kill us? Plus, he's been way too nice. He seems kind of fishy."

"Shhhhh. He may be able to hear us."

"Okay, fine, but-"

"Just stop, Theo. I'm sick of you treating me like I don't know what I'm doing. It's hard enough for me every day, needing to find the motivation to get up every morning. I don't need your unreal expectations weighing me down too."

"Is that how you really feel?" Theo asked, and he looked genuinely hurt.

"I suppose I do," I said looking away.

"I'm sorry. I've just been on edge lately. I guess I didn't realize I was doing it."

"It's okay," I whispered.

He came and sat on the edge of the bed next to me where I had sat myself down.

He wrapped his arms around me and whispered again, "I'm sorry. I will do better. I don't want to lose you, just like I lost someone else."

I looked up at him, and he could see the question in my eyes.

"There is one thing I didn't tell you in that hotel."

# 11

"Oh?" I said.

"When I was eighteen, I had already been working with Queen Aria for around two years. There was a bioscience girl, Remi was her name. Beautiful girl, strawberry blonde, light blue eyes, one of the kindest girls I'd met. We became friends and, around a year later, she was my girlfriend. We had been happily dating for three years, and I was the happiest man alive. I was planning to propose to her but, a week before I was going to, something happened. Remi's sister, Amy, had just turned twenty, and she had failed her test. Remi tried to get her to escape, but she was caught. Then, before I knew it, the love of my life was taken away from me, and sentenced to death for committing treason against the Queen. She was killed by a firing squad," he finished in one big breath, and his face was red, with tears pooling in his eyes. Then, it was my turn to comfort him, sliding my arms around him into a hug,

"I'm so sorry. I guess I didn't realize. We just have to remember, everyone is fighting a battle that everyone else is oblivious to. We just have to learn to talk to each other."

"I'm sorry for getting mad at you earlier," he quietly said.

"I'm sorry too."

I felt better now that I had talked with Theo. I felt as if I knew where he was coming from. "I think I'll go to bed now," I said to Theo, curling up on my twin-sized bed, and pulling the covers up to my shoulders. Before I knew it, I was drifting off into sleep, as peaceful as ever.

I woke up to the sound of muffled voices. I stood up groggily, my eyes still heavy. I pressed my ear against the door.

"What's wrong with you!" I heard a voice shriek from downstairs.

"What's wrong with me? You're the one who came into MY house and started questioning me! I've done nothing wrong."

It was Theo and Kohl.

Before I knew it, my feet were moving swiftly down the stairs. I walked into the living room to find them standing up face to face.

"Oh! Maria," Theo muttered.

"What are you doing!" I cried. "You promised, Theo! You promised not to do this. We're each fighting our own battles, remember?" Theo backed away from Kohl. As far as I can tell, nothing got physical, but only the gods knew.

"Are you hurt?" I asked them both but directed the message to Kohl.

"No," they both mumbled.

"Good. I'm so sorry, Kohl. I think that Theo has something to say," I glared at him.

"I'm sorry," Theo said, in a very unbelievable voice.

"It's fine," Kohl replied, sitting on the sofa.

I sighed. I suppose that was that.

Theo and I fought again that night. But, this time, it was outside of Kohl's house, in the parking lot.

"Why do I keep having to watch you like you're a little boy!" I asked him. "You're better than that."

"You don't have to watch me! I know how to take care of myself."

"But, that's the thing, I do have to watch you. If I don't ,you'd probably kill Kohl!"

"At least he'd be dead!" he retorted.

Well, that one stung. "You don't understand how hard it is," I mumbled under my breath.

"Just kill him already. Do it now before you get more attached than you already are."

"I can't!"

"But you can. Come on, Maria, just kill the poor excuse of a thief. Don't get all sentimental. That was all a long time ago."

"FINE!" I shouted, finally unable to take any more of the weight that was being barred on my shoulders. At that moment, I felt like Atlas from the old stories, commanded to carry the weight of the world forever. But if I could eliminate just one target, then eternity would end.

"I'll do it tonight," I whispered to Theo. "But, in the meantime, just leave me alone."

He put a hand on my shoulder as I turned my back to walk to the door.'

"Don't forget about me when you finally are free," he begged.

"I'll try not to."

# 12

Tonight was the perfect time for a murder. The sky was a dark stormy gray, and it was thunder storming, giving the extra dramatic effect of doom.

After I had wished a good night to Kohl, Theo and I wandered upstairs and waited in our small guest bedroom. I listened to the pitter-patter of the rain until the sound of Kohl's footsteps echoed through the vacant hallway. Then I waited again, the lulling sound of the rain almost making me fall asleep until the booming claps of thunder woke me again. Around midnight, I got up off the bed and told Theo to stay here. It was go time. He nodded his head silently and watched me gather my dagger, a suitable weapon for murder. It was a custom-made one, a gift from the Queen when I was first admitted into my job. It was a black leather handle with a one-and-a-half-foot ivory blade. It was my favorite dagger. I poked the end, and it was as sharp as ever. I quietly opened my door and creeped out into the hallway.

Without sound, I opened the door to Kohl's room. It was a rather plain room, with just his single double bed, pushed up against the wall in the left corner of the room. There wasn't even a dresser, just a small door that I assumed was a closet. The walls were a fine light gray, and the floors the same mahogany as the ones downstairs. There was, however, a desk, with heaping piles of papers. I'll admit, I was tempted to look at them, but resisted the urge and got back to the matter at hand. There he was, sound asleep, without a care in the world. He was asleep on his back, making him the perfect target. I raised my dagger, smack dab in where the middle of his heart would be. I was about to bring it down, but I paused. I couldn't do it. I sat like that for a good while, dagger raised over his back, waiting patiently to taste the blood of another victim. After a while of standing like that over his bed, he woke up.

"What are you doing?" he asked, and the fear in his eyes is what made me break.

The dagger fell to the ground and I collapsed onto the bed, balling. I was glad the door was closed or Theo would have heard.

"What's wrong? What were you doing?" he asked, trying to comfort me, yet still a little scared.

I couldn't help but tell him everything.

I told him how I was the Queen's personal assassin, how I was a murderer, and how I was scared of myself. I told him that I was supposed to kill him because he stole from the Queen, an act of treason in her eyes. I told him how I couldn't do it. I told him how Theo was really a guard and why we had the fight the day that we met. I even told him about how I murdered in cold blood his brother, Charlie. I just let the words spill out, an overflow of mixed emotions. Despite the rage I thought he must be feeling, he spoke to me softly, holding me in his arms to keep me from doing anything drastic.

"It's okay," he whispered. "We will have a lot to talk about but, for now, you're okay."

"No, no, I'm not."

"It's okay. I don't view you any differently. I was bound to ask you how you're not with the Queen now, anyway. I was one of the lucky people who got out of it, you know, that was the only good thing that came out of moving." I looked up into his calming blue eyes and it was like getting lost in the ocean. I bottled those feelings up, though. There was no way he'd want to continue being my friend.

"I don't care what you say. Opinions can change, Kohl. My number one fear right now is that you will start to view me the way I view myself, a murderer," I fearfully whispered that into his ear. He didn't reply.

"What will I do about Theo?" I asked, the tears on my face starting to dry. "He's bound to try to kill you, maybe even me. I can't go back in there," I told him, fear and panic rising inside of me.

"Take a deep breath," he said, his dark rich voice calm as ever. "You're going to tell him exactly what I say, are you ready?"

I nodded.

"You're going to go back in that room, don't show any fear, or anger. Then you're going to say, no luck. He wasn't there. I went downstairs and looked too. He must have gone out. Then, just as a precaution, I'll go for a little walk outside, okay? Now, go, he won't hurt you and, so, god help me, if he does… " He didn't finish the last part. I brushed the hair out of my face and picked up the weapon. I struggled to help Kohl out of the window, and then he was off, into the stormy darkness.

# 13

I did as Kohl had advised me to do, and took a few deep breaths before exiting his room into the hallway. I creaked open the door to our room, and there Theo sat, awake as ever.

"So?" he said, hopping up onto his feet. I recited what Kohl had said.

"No, no, luck. He wasn't there. I went downstairs and looked too. He must have gone out."

The light in Theo's eyes flickered out.

"You're sure?" he asked.

"Positive. But you're free to check the house,." I told him.

And he did just that; checking every door, crack, crevice, and dark corner. Nothing.

"Are you kidding me!" he made an angry grunt. Then he took a deep breath. "I suppose we have nowhere else to be, so anytime could work." He stomped back upstairs and slammed the door behind him. I would give him his own space. I didn't sleep the rest of the night.

In the morning, Theo didn't come out of his room. I didn't push it, either.

"Do you want to go get some breakfast?" I asked Kohl.

"Why not? We need to have a chat anyway."

I forgot about that. Oh, well, it would be awkward but it needed to happen.

We walked to a local restaurant called The Breakfast Bowl.

We sat at our table for two and placed our orders on these screens that were at our table.

"So, where would you like to start?" I asked.

"From the beginning. Why does she want me dead?" he asked.

"Well, she said that you were an ex guard who stole a lot of money from her. And that was treason. So, I guess that's why."

Kohl just shook his head, not in a good way, in a, wait, what do you mean? way.

"I've never worked for the Queen," he said.

"What!"

"I've never worked for her, let alone stolen money."

My brain drew a blank. Did she lie to me?

"Oh," was all I managed to say.

"Okay, we can tackle that later. Let's move on to the next thing," Kohl says.

"What else do you want to know?"

"Tell me a little bit about Theo," he urged. "He intrigues me and I'm not sure if it's in a good way."

I tried to spend a good portion on Theo. "Well, he's been a guard for, I think, around 1elevenyears?" I said, trying to jog my memory to the best of my ability. "He said he cares for me… he had a girlfriend, but she died. I don't know what else there is to say."

Kohl paused. "Can you tell me why he hates me so much?"

I guess that caught me off guard. "I didn't know he hated you," I tried to sound convincing but he didn't buy it.

"Don't lie. I won't be mad," he promised, reaching his hand across the table to take mine. "I won't be mad."

"Well, he just thinks you're a bad person, I guess. He has anger issues I didn't really know about until now. He's concerned that, if I don't kill you, I'll be killed. I guess he's just fueled by that," I finished off, just as the waitress came to drop off our food, for me, a stack of chocolate chip pancakes with thick, buttery maple syrup. For Kohl, a breakfast bowl, with spinach, eggs, bacon, avocado, and many other good foods.

Kohl ignored the food and shook his head solemnly.

"If you needed to, you could always just kill me anyway," he whispered, face dark.

"Absolutely not," I replied, so fast that I barely understood what I said.

He started to speak but I cut him off.

"Kohl, we've been friends for so long, even if we didn't know it, we still thought about each other. There's another option, I'm sure of it." That was that, and he knew I wouldn't take another answer. I cut into my stack of three pancakes and took a bite.

"Anything else?" I asked.

"I can completely understand if you'd rather not talk about this. It has to hurt. But what about Charlie?"

I winced in my head.

"I didn't mean to kill him. I didn't want to kill him. But he was holding us back from finding you, which was my main goal. I wish that I could go back and undo what I did," I softly said, then said in my head, sometimes I wish I was that girl.

He nodded his head.

"I don't blame you, you know. It's something you had to do."

"I didn't have to do anything. I chose to kill him to make it easier to find you."

I uncomfortably smooshed my food around on my plate, the pancakes didn't look so appetizing anymore.

"I still don't blame you. Just tell me, was it too painful?"

I thought back to the moment I had tried to block out.

"It was quick," I said in a low breathy voice. "I don't know about painless. Knife to the throat," I added softly.

He just nodded his head, almost sympathetically.

He took a bite of his food, showing not much emotion on his face.

"What do you plan on doing?" he asked.

"I don't know," I said, being blatantly honest.

"There's not many options. For now, just lay low."

"I can't," I replied. "I'd love to stay with you but I'm scared that Theo will kill you either way."

I looked into his ocean-like eyes, and I felt like I was drowning in their sorrow. I knew what he'd say once more.

"Then let him. I've had a life. You only know this. You deserve it more than anyone."

He kept urging me on with that thought, a swirling pool of darkness clouding my thoughts.

"I can't." That's when I realized that maybe Kohl was going through something, too.

"Are you okay?" I asked.

"No," he whispered.

"What's wrong?" I asked. It seemed like a silly question. Of course, everything was wrong.

"Everything," he replied, proving my point.

"First, everything was great, I met my best friend after a long time apart, but then I found out she's being forced to kill me; what a bummer. But, then, I also find out her acquaintance, friend, or whatever, may or may not be a psychopathic pusher. To top it all off, that's all when I'm grieving for my brother, who was murdered. It's a lot, Maria. And it's not all your fault. It's just stressful, I don't know what to do." He dragged his hand down his face, giving a big sigh.

"I know, it was a stupid question."

He sighed and took a bite of his now cold food. "It's fine."

After we had a talk, we paid our bill and decided to go on a walk through Timberland Park, Genoa's biggest. It was mid-morning, and the breeze was tranquil and smelled of fresh bread. We didn't start talking until we found a bench underneath a large oak to sit on.

"I have an idea," Kohl whispered so quietly I wasn't sure if he'd actually said a word.

"What is it?"

His answer was so, so soft, but the park was quiet, and the breeze carried on his message.

"What if we kill the Queen."

# 14

At first, I thought I heard him wrong.

"What?" I asked, far too bewildered to speak.

"I said, what if we killed the Queen."

He wasn't looking at me anymore, his back was turned, facing the sprawling park filled with oak and sycamore trees.

I truly didn't mean to sound rude, or snappy. But it just slipped out.

"Are you mad? I'd be killed for bringing you alive on campus, you'd be killed on sight! If we did manage to get in, we wouldn't make it anywhere near the Queen."

"It is a long shot," he agreed. "But this could all be over." He had turned back to face me, his voice was filled with longing. "Forever," he whispered. "Children will no longer be scared to grow up, adults will never be murdered in cold blood on the cold floors of Castle Marion. It will all be over." His voice was almost begging. He had scooted closer to me, his hands resting on my shoulders.

I pressed into him, letting my mind think.

"Do you think you'll ever have children?" I asked silently.

"Maybe," he replies. "But I'd need to find the right girl, first. Someone brave, strong, kind, and loving. Yet beautiful to me and, even when the world rejects me, she will still love me. A girl like that," he says softly.

I continuously kept those words in my head and I realized I had a future ahead of me. It would be hard and risky. Surely Theo wouldn't approve. But I'm sick of worrying about what other people think, or want.

I sat up on the hard park bench. "Let's do it."

"It's going to be hard," I said, "But nothing we can't do."

Kohl beamed at me. "Thank you," he said, his voice wobbly. "It means a lot."

I just nodded my head but continued right on with the next issue.

"First, we need to find out why the Queen wants you killed."

The light slowly faded out of Kohl's eyes, but I could see the gears in his head thinking. That's when he let out a sigh, but not a sigh of relief.

"I think I know why." He waited for a response but I said nothing, just motioning for him to continue.

"You see, my father, Robert, used to be very high up in the government. Some sort of political status. He petitioned, against the Queen, to have the placing ceremony discontinued. He, of course, got thousands of votes. For obvious reasons, this was a terrible ordeal for the Queen. She ordered his death but, because of his status, he was untouchable, even by the Queen herself. It's a year later that we moved. My dad feared for my safety and, I suppose, for a good reason."

That made a lot of sense.

"So, that's why she wants you dead! She can't touch your dad, so she gets to you. Smart on her end, but why did she wait until now? There has to be something bigger going on," I said. I thought back to all of the previous things she'd said.

I was the first assassin in years... she was waiting for me.

"I was the first assassin in years,' the Queen said. The Queen was waiting for me," I said, repeating my thoughts.

I saw the puzzle pieces click together in his head, and he nodded.

"That does make more sense than whatever we were thinking before," he agreed.

There was an awkward stretch of silence between us, until I finally said, "We should be getting back to your house. We need to act naturally so Theo doesn't suspect anything."

He nodded, and rose from the park bench, giving me his hand to pull me up.

The walk back was long and draining. There was a sudden mood shift in the air as if our most recent conversation had dampened the spirit of the world.

The Queen's words still rang in my head, a constant reminder of what should have already happened. An image of the girl's lifeless body floated around there too. My head was light and airy, and my knees were starting to shake.

"Hey, Kohl. I think I need to sit down," I said it so softly, my voice was frail. Then, before I knew it, everything went black.

## 15

I was roughly aware of what was going on around me. Kohl stood over me, a few bystanders approaching me but, while in the back of my head, I knew this was happening, I still wasn't there. It was almost like my dream, soaring through the clouds. That's how I felt at that moment like nothing could stop me, but then slowly, I'd start to fall, just to rise again. Maybe I was just going in and out of consciousness, but that's not what my brain saw. It saw stars, rainbows, and happy thoughts. Soon enough, it all went black again.

I came too in Kohl's bedroom. He and Theo are on the side of my bed. A cold compress was on my forehead.

"You're okay!" Theo breathed a sigh of relief. He pulled me in for a hug, and I tried to hug him back.

"What happened?" I asked my head still too foggy to process what happened.

"We aren't quite sure. They wanted to bring you to the hospital but I told them to leave it. I know it's not what you'd want," he said, choosing his words carefully, he knew that it wasn't time to tell Theo everything.

"I still find that a rather odd choice," Theo noted, adding, "I'd still take her to the hospital."

Kohl paused before saying, "I definitely contemplated it but couldn't have carried her, and I didn't have my cell."

"It's just a shame," Theo said, his voice oily.

Kohl rose from the side of the bed, and walked over to the door, standing in the frame. His back was pressed against the side of the doorframe. He closed his eyes and tried to smile.

"Why, yes, it is, isn't it." Then he was out the door. A slamming sound from downstairs followed suit.

Theo stayed put, not leaving my side.

"Are you okay?" he asked. "It was a jerk move not to bring you to the hospital, if you ask me."

"I'm fine," I replied. "I just want to know what happened."

"Well, Remi knew quite a bit about the human body. This happened to the head of the Science Division. No one could figure out what was wrong with him. Devan Rodgers, I believe his name was. Remi was able to figure out that he was very stressed, causing him to faint. Who knows if that's what happened to you? We're thinking that's what happened though. But, in the meantime, do you have anything to talk about?"

I knew what he was hinting at, anything stressful I may have been hiding. I just replied, "Not particularly."

I sat up and scooted to the edge of Kohl's bed. I put my feet on the floor and stood. I tested out my legs first, making sure I was stable before taking my first step.

"Careful," Theo winced, grasping my shoulder at the slight sight of a wobble.

"Thanks," I smiled and hoped I didn't sound bitter. He seemed to be in a better mood, at least with me. But I still couldn't ignore the fact that he pushed me to do things I clearly didn't want to do.

"Please don't be mad," he whispered into my ear as I walked to the door.

He tangled his arms around my back, hugging me, and I had to resist the urge to pull away.

"I'm not mad," I promised, and this time I knew he believed me, even if I wasn't sure I believed myself.

# 16

Theo didn't look at me as he softly said, "Okay."

I smiled, knowing that my face had to be brighter than his.

This time, he didn't stop me as I walked out of the door, but he did say, "Remember what we came here for. Don't get too attached, I can't stand to see your heart broken."

I didn't reply.

I went to go find Khol, and I didn't plan on telling him what had happened. I didn't feel a thing, not one ounce of love for that man. But, somehow, I knew I had to do it in order to get him to let me leave. Kohl was nowhere to be found in the house and, so, remembering the slamming door, I walked outside to find Kohl sitting on the steps.

"Hey," I said, slinking down next to him.

"Hey."

There was an uncomfortable silence until I filled it by asking, "So, what are you up to?"

"Just thinking."

Something was very off about him, but I didn't want to just keep prodding him. I know how that feels, and it's not very good.

He seemed to realize I noticed, and I wasn't going to be one of those friends who walked out on you when you needed them most, so, instead, I sat there, waiting for him to say something, anything.

"I just feel like the whole world is against me, you know?" he finally answered in a meek voice.

I nodded, letting him know I was listening.

"I feel like all Theo wants to do is play devil's advocate, and I'm so sick of it. My brother has passed, Theo hates me, and the world hates me," he said it all so quietly I know he had hoped I didn't hear him. But I heard every word.

"I don't hate you, Kohl. What you need to realize is you should always be yourself, because every other single person on this earth already exists. That is special to me, and to all the other people in your life who you care about."

"I suppose," he mumbled.

I faced him and placed both hands on his shoulders.

"I don't suppose, I know."

We only stayed on those steps a moment longer before we stood up and Kohl turned to me and said, "I'm going on a walk. I'd rather be alone right now. Just shout if anything happens."

I respected his wish and asked him to be careful as I wandered inside.

While he was away, I might as well create some sort of plan. But, right now, Theo was home, so it was too risky. In the end, I decided it was a risk I was willing to take.

I ran up the stairs, ignoring Theo who had said something to me from the living room. I entered Kohl's room and grabbed a stack of blank paper from his desk and a pen.

I exited and sat on my bed and, just as my pen touched the paper, there was a knock at the door as Theo stuck his head in.

"Are you okay? What are you doing?"

"Just doodling," I replied, holding up a hastily scribbled cat.

"Oh, okay." He looked slightly disappointed but didn't say anything else as he walked back downstairs.

With that, I began to work. I brainstormed, writing down anything that could be used to help us on our mission. That's when I thought of a wonderful idea.

I scribbled down the word PLAN on the right side of the paper where I hadn't written anything. Then I began to write.

"I was thinking about what I remembered from the castle. It's been about two weeks since I left. My room cleaner, Jackie, was a wonderful woman. Middle-aged, short curly brown hair and green eyes. A lovely woman with a kind wife and an adoptive son, Brandon. What if I could somehow manage to talk to her, get her a letter or message? Once I'm inside, I can get the information about what has been happening. She can tell me more about the Queen's plans. I don't know if I dare tell her mine. For now, that is what I will do."

I finished up my paragraph, and piled a bunch of blank papers on top of it, finishing with my cat on top. I hid it in the bottom of my bag, hoping Theo didn't come across it.

I wandered back downstairs and sat next to Theo on the sofa. It was late afternoon, maybe around one p.m.

Things were very quiet, so I picked a magazine up from the table titled, "Fashion and Flames. What happens when you combine the two?"

I flipped through the pages, looking through images of drop-dead gorgeous women dressed in flame-inspired outfits. One woman, with coffee brown skin and long flowing hair, had a burnt orange dress with a slit going up one side of the thigh. Another woman with flawless white skin was dressed in a poppy red dress that was ruffled at the bottom with a fiery orangish yellow cape. The magazine was mostly women, but it also showcased a couple of men, as well, showing off their femininity.

One man, with dark blonde hair and tan skin, was dressed in a bright yellow tuxedo, with an orangish undershirt and a tie with flames. The other man was dressed in a bright red off-the-shoulder dress with these high black platform boots. The magazine was interesting, and I enjoyed seeing how people, even men, expressed themselves through their clothing and had their free will as every individual should.

"So, how are you doing?" Theos' voice broke through the silence.

"I'm fine, I guess. Kind of sick of this city, and this house." And maybe even the people, I added in my head.

"I can agree with that. I've been rather lonely, to be honest. You haven't been around much," he mumbled.

I had to admit, I had spent most of my time with Kohl. Maybe I felt a slight twinge of guilt for not being around much. I was supposed to be here with Theo.

"I'm sorry."

"It's not your fault. You were just trying to find ways to do your job. I just haven't been much help."

"Yeah," I replied. "Just trying to do my job."

I looked up from my magazine and glanced at Theo. He looked sad. I don't know why I pitied this man so much. I saw him as nothing more than a friend, yet it was as if something was drawing my attention to him.

He looked over at me and said, "Would you like to watch the sunset tonight?"

"Of course."

# 17

Later that night, I climbed up the ladder ,to the roof and found Theo sitting there silently. I sat crisscrossed next to him.

"Hey" Theo announced when he heard me.

"Hey."

I sat next to him on the cold concrete.

The sky was like a thousand glowing embers painting the world above warm palettes of orange and pink and yellow.

"The sky is beautiful today," he murmured.

"Yes, yes, it is." He looked at the sky, then at me.

"The main reason I asked you to come here was so that we could talk."My forehead started to sweat.

"What about?" I asked.

"Well, I just feel like everything has been off lately. We were a team, but now you disappear for hours with Kohl, or by yourself. I know I already asked but, this time, I want the truth. Are you okay?"

I obviously couldn't tell him the truth, he would go ballistic. Instead, I worked around the truth, not telling him lies, but not revealing the truth.

"The truth is, I've been extremely stressed. I'm trying to make plans about my job, and how to do it easily, quickly, and relatively painlessly." He shook his head solemnly.

"I understand that. Do… Do you want me to do it for you?"

Before I had time to think about what I was going to say, I blurted out, "NO!"

Immediately, I regretted my decision, knowing that he'd wonder why I said it so abruptly.

"I mean, no. I didn't mean to shout it. I already have a plan in the works, so I just didn't want to tell you."

"Well, let's hear it."

I wasn't lying, I did have a plan. Not the way he was thinking though.

"It's not finalized. I promise I will let you know as soon as it is finished."

He didn't seem to like that answer, and he rubbed the nape of his neck.

"You promise? No matter what, we're in this together," Theo said, in an almost begging tone.

"I promise," I answered.

The following morning was extra bright. The weather was far too nice to sit inside all day. Kohl was waiting for me with a scalding hot cup of coffee. Theo was still asleep upstairs.

"Good morning," he said, putting his coffee down and picking up mine.

"Good morning," I replied, taking the cup of coffee I was offered.

"Feeling any better?" I asked.

"Much better. Thanks for asking. Yesterday was very tense. Well, I have some good news."

"Yeah? What is it?" he asked.

"Not here," I told him.

He took the hint and we got up and walked to the front door, where we went outside and sat on the steps. I held my warm cup, its contents warming my hands.

"So, what is it?" Kohl asked again.

I pulled out the paper with my plans; I had grabbed it before leaving the guest room.

I handed them to Kohl and, as he read them, I also voiced my idea.

"Back at Castle Marion, my room cleaner and I were fairly close. I was thinking we could get a letter to her somehow. Find out what's happening."

"That's a good idea, actually. But what if the Queen sees it or, worse, reads it?" he asks, glancing back down at the paper.

"We'd have to find a way to encrypt it," I replied.

We take a minute to think, then he says, "I've got it! It's rather simple, actually. But it may just work. What if each letter was where it was in the alphabet? Like A is one, B is two, and so on. Your name would be 13 1 18 9 1. It may be a little hard, but I'm sure she's a smart woman."

"That's an amazing idea!" I cried, throwing my arms around him. It surprised him, but he wrapped himself around me.

"We're doing it," I whispered in his ear.

"Soon, this will merely be a memory," he promised.

We headed back inside. Theo was still nowhere to be seen, which was expected. We had until at least eleven a.m. That gave us around two hours to get what we needed to be done.

"I'll be right back," says Kohl. "I'm going to get some lined paper for the letter."

He vanished up the stairs and returned no more than a minute later.

We sat at the counter, the alphabet written out on a separate sheet, with its corresponding number written underneath. This wasn't to put in the letter, but more so to make it easier to write.

We had finally finished it, and I read it over to make sure it was what I needed it to be.

"Dear Jackie,

Hello! How have you been? I've been okay. This may be a lot to read and, whatever you do, I beg you not to report me to the Queen. A lot has happened since I left almost two and a half weeks ago. I need inside information on what has been happening at Castle Marion. I know there is only so much you can give me, and don't jeopardize your or your family's safety. Tell Lily I said hello.

Your friend,
Maria."

Now that it was all encoded, we were ready to send. I grabbed the envelope sitting proudly on the table and neatly folded our message. On the back, I wrote, "8778 Castle Marion, Chester, Avion." I slapped a stamp with a phoenix on it. The phoenix was a bird everyone was familiar with; it had fiery orange feathers and long delicate feathers. But Avion isn't hot all year long; places like that are where phoenix usually decide to make their homes. No one knows how it came to be, but Avion is home to the white p,hoenix, the only continent where they live. They have snow-white feathers with piercing blue eyes, most of the time. In the summer they fade to a light orange.

"Ready to go?" Kohl asked.

"Yes," I replied, and ran to the door, opening it. I could barely contain my excitement as I ran to the nearest postal box, little wooden containers where you could drop the post and, every day at five p.m., the couriers come and pick it up.

I dropped it in and walked back to Kohl's.

"Now, we wait."

# 18

About a week and a half later I got the letter. It was in a bright white envelope, sealed with a crimson red wax seal. I was eager to open it, but I had to wait for Theo to leave the room. We were all sitting in the living room watching a movie, maybe even getting along. I brought in the letter and set it face down on the counter.

"Just a bill," I said, and dismissed it before a conversation could start.

After the movie had ended, Theo declared he was going out for lunch.

"Would you like to tag along?" he asked Kohl and me, but directed the question mostly to me.

"Not this time," I told him. I rubbed my eyes and then held my stomach. "I have a killer headache. And a bit of a stomach ache."

"Oh. That's fine. I hope that you feel better; get some rest. I'll bring you back some soup."

"Thank you," I regarded him with a tight hug.

"Any time."

Once I heard the door close, I turned to Kohl.

"We got our letter," I say.

His eyes shone with excitement. "That's what I was hoping for."

I walked over to the letter and picked it up. We sat on the sofa, huddled next to each other, with him watching me opening the letter.

I peeled off the wax seal and carefully pulled out the uncrinkled paper.

It was in the code we wrote it in, so I grabbed my deciphering sheet.

Kohl read it out loud, "Meet me at Timberland Park on May seventh at three p.m."

There wasn't a name or return address. Of course, I knew who it was from, but it seemed hastily written. I hope nothing happened.

"What's today's date?" I asked.

Kohl yanked the newspaper out from underneath the pile of books on his coffee table.

"May seventh," he replied, his eyes wide.

I glanced at the clock on the wall. It read two-thirty p.m.

"We have to get going! We will be late to our best source of information," I urged. Timberland Park was around a fifteen-minute walk, so we should get there with enough time to spare.

Before I knew it, we were on our way to the park, walking at a very brisk pace, but not quite running. Soon enough, we saw the large arch of the park. Timberland Park stretches about a mile and a half. There is a good portion of land, so where could she be? We wandered the park, looking for the short, curly-haired woman who held all of the information we needed. I was almost losing hope, until I saw her; she was dressed in a red button-up cardigan.

"Jackie!" I called out to her.

She looked up at me, but her face was full of sorrow. She stood up and brushed the grass off of her jeans.

Kohl approached her first, shaking her hand.

"Nice to meet you, I'm Kohl."

"So I've heard," she replied.

"Are you okay, Jackie?" I asked her this question because the usual soft melody of her voice was gone, replaced by worry.

"No, I'm not. And neither are you."

I backed up a step.

"What do you mean, I'm not? I feel fine, I'm happy for once," I replied.

She rubs her temples and wanders over to sit down on a hickory park bench.

"You'd better sit down. This is going to be a long story."

There wasn't much room on the bench, not for three people, so I sat on the grass, my knees pulled up to my chest. Kohl sat next to me, giving Jackie room to comfortably sprawl out.

"Before you ask, no, the Queen did not read the letter, nor figure it out. I collect the post for her so I wasn't worried about that." I breathed a sigh of relief and crossed that off my list of worries. Sadly, it seemed like a million more were still floating through my brain.

"You see, the Queen was talking about you the other day. She said that you'd been gone a long time. She says if you don't return by May ninth, she's sending someone out to look for you." She took a breath and paused. "She also has some suspicions. She thinks that because you have been gone for almost a month, you may have switched sides. This meeting is proof her thoughts are true. Now listen to me, very carefully. You are not safe here. She will find you and, when she does find you, she will not be happy. I'd advise you to find somewhere else to go."

"This is a lot of information," I replied. "But there is a slight issue. I have a guard with me, Theo Bremuta. I don't think he'd take kindly to this. A very devoted boy, he is."

She stopped to think for a minute. "That does complicate things. What if you lied to him, said you were going to report back to the Queen to see how things went?"

"That could work," I say, "But that's at least a day and a half worth of walking."

"Then don't walk. I'm sure we could find you a car. It would be too risky for you to come back with me." She pointed at Kohl. "Do you have a car?" she asked.

"Sadly, I don't. But, even if I did, this plan isn't the greatest. Don't you think it would appear a little suspicious if Maria just showed up out of nowhere, right before the deadline? I sure think it would. Plus, they'd ask questions, and questions are never good. They would question Theo and Maria and, if their lies don't match up, then they will be caught."

Jackie nodded solemnly. "I didn't even think of that. We have to come up with something bigger, something better," she said, rubbing her forehead.

No one said anything for a while; we all thought, our brains working as one. We'd get occasional ideas just to have them shot down by another fault in their works.

That was until a lightbulb went off in my head. It wasn't shining bright like I would have liked, but it wasn't dwindling out either. It was a low light but, with some help, it may just grow brighter.

"What if we took the information that we have overall, not just here, and first gathered it? So, our ultimate goal is to eliminate Queen Aria. So far, we have learned that she wishes Kohl dead because she cannot get to his father. We have learned that she is growing suspicious of me. Combining our knowledge of that, we can find out that she is very impatient. I think the next thing we need to do is-" I was cut off by a scream in the distance. I glanced over at the gate and that's when I saw it. In the far distance, were three men riding black Friesian horses. The exact kind that the Queen owns.

# 19

I froze right where I was standing. My heart was pounding loud in my ears, threatening to explode out of my chest.

"Jackie," I whispered, still not daring to move.

She didn't even look at me, she just peered through the trees, knowing what I was hinting at.

Kohl looked at me and I nodded. He stood up and disappeared back in the direction of his house. I no longer heard screams, but I heard the click-clack of horse hooves nearing, at a fast pace. I stood up and started walking deeper into the park. Jackie followed suit and, as the click-clack grew louder, we moved faster.

Jackie must have been almost as clueless as to where we were going as I was because, as we twisted and turned over the mile-and-a-half-long park, it seemed as if we were getting lost in a tangle of trees. The occasional person was walking around, but most people were at lunch, or an early dinner. We came out on the other side of the park, walking into South Genoa. The streets were calm, and the smell of fresh bread and newly-cut roses danced around my nose. The clicking of the horses had long faded, but there was still an issue. They were here, and they were here for me. Everything about my situation was looking grim. I can't be found wandering around the streets of Genoa with Jackie, that would get us both in trouble. Maybe even killed. But I couldn't be seen huddled in a circle with Jackie and Kohl. Kohl would be shot on the spot. We probably all would. It was of no use trying to run. If I was to have a chance, I have to stop being so weak. I'm supposed to be an assassin, and I feel as if I'm everything but that. I am going to kill Queen Aria anyway, aren't I? What's the difference with adding a few guards into the mix? I have to admit, I'd feel guilty, but I already have so much guilt weighing me down that another sprinkle more wouldn't make a difference in the long run.

Jackie turns to me.

"What are we going to do?" she asks, her ears were bright red and her eyes had tears gathering at the waterline.

"Well, I can't tell you what we should do, but I can tell you what we shouldn't," I say. "We should stay away from the northern side of Genoa. And we cannot go back to Kohl's house."

She nods, breathing in deeply, and exhaling slowly.

We continue walking down the street, finding little shops and street vendors on the rather calm roads. There were still cars hustling about but, compared to the northern end, it was quite tranquil. It wasn't too loud, it didn't smell like hot trash or body odor.

"Where should we go?" Jackie whispers to no one in particular.

I don't answer, because I don't have an answer.

We wander the streets for what feels like an eternity, stopping occasionally to take a break. We continued walking until we came upon something peculiar. A group of people huddled together in a circle. People looked frantic and unsure. There was a lot of shouting and people waving their hands around. I heard sirens in the distance. Jackie and I approached briskly, wondering what could have happened.

"Is everyone okay?" I shout, hoping one of the several people encasing the mystery before us would hear me.

"No," a woman with ginger hair whips around and says. Her voice sounded heavy and her face was a shiny pink.

With a solemn face, she steps to the side revealing the injured man before us. It took me until the bright white ambulance with flashy lights pulled up to the curb to realize that the injured man was Kohl.

## 20

As I approached the scene, my mind struggled to comprehend what I was seeing. Kohl was lying on the ground, his body still and lifeless. A man was bent over him, pressing a makeshift compress against his stomach in an attempt to stop the bleeding. In a flash, I was at Kohl's side, searching for any sign of life. But Jackie, who had been with me moments before, had vanished into the throng of people and was nowhere to be found. Perhaps it was for the best; I wouldn't have been able to pay attention to her anyways, as all of my focus was on Kohl.

"Kohl," I whispered into his ear, hoping for a response. His beautiful green eyes flickered over to me, and I saw a glimmer of recognition in their depths. He weakly squeezed my hand, and I felt a wave of relief wash over me. But my relief was short-lived as the paramedics pushed their way through the crowd, barking orders and instructions.

"Ma'am, I'm going to have to ask you to step back," one of them said to me firmly.

"I-I can't leave him!" I protested, not making any move to comply with their request. The paramedics looked at me quizzically, trying to determine my relationship with

Kohl. "Are you related in any way? Girlfriend, sister, aunt, mother?"

"Not exactly," I replied, "But we are very close. We've been friends for over fifteen years." I could see the hesitation in their eyes, but, eventually, they nodded and allowed me to stay. As they removed the compress, I saw the full extent of Kohl's injury: a deep, oozing stab wound in his stomach, the edges blackened and infected. I gasped and turned away, unable to bear the sight. I heard them pour a stinging antiseptic onto the wound and saw Kohl flinch slightly at the pain. He looked at me, his eyes full of fear and pain, as they lifted him onto a stretcher and loaded him into the ambulance. I didn't know what to do as they sped off, taking Kohl away from me. Slowly but surely, the crowd began to dissipate, leaving me alone on the sidewalk, still in shock and too stunned to move. I felt a tap on my shoulder and turned to see Jackie standing there, her face etched with concern.

"Take a deep breath," she said, pulling me into a long hug. I was so upset that I couldn't even cry.

"Why don't you go back to the castle, okay? I need some time to go make sure Kohl's okay. I won't be as focused if you are here." I don't even apologize for being rude.

She just nodded her head.

"Good luck," she called, as she walked down the street in the direction of Castle Marion.

As soon as she was off, I started walking in the opposite direction, to the hospital where Kohl had been taken. I started at a walk, but, by the time I got there, I was at a full sprint. I wiped the sweat from my forehead and opened the door to go inside. I was blasted with that classic hospital smell, the one that no one can describe, but everyone knows what it smells like. I walked across the white tiled floors to the woman at the front desk.

"Hello, sweetheart. How can I help you?" she asks, looking up from her laptop. She was an older woman, with a loose gray bun and soft brown eyes, and the kindest smile I'd seen in a while.

"Hello," I said to her. "I was wondering if I could see Kohl Scott? He was an emergency case picked up on West Richard Street just a short while ago."

"Let me look that up for you."

She types something into her computer.

"Oh, dear, I'm so sorry. He is here but he's not allowed any visitations yet. It will be quite a while; he's in surgery right now. Maybe a few days. You're welcome to wait here, though. It may be sooner."

"Thank you," I whisper. "Thank you so much."

Twenty-six hours. That is how long I was in that hospital. I sat in the waiting room the whole time, as people came in and out. The receptionist, whose name I learned was Fran, even brought me some food from the cafeteria. It wasn't too great, but it kept something in my stomach. I was staring off into space when Fran called my name.

"Maria, honey. You can go see him now." I shook my head, getting me out of whatever trance I was in. I jumped up and nearly skipped to her desk. "Here's your visitation pass," she said, handing me a slip of paper. "His room will be number one twenty-five, on the third floor."

"Thank you so much," I replied, graciously taking the piece of paper with his room information on it.

"Any time, dear. Do tell him I hope he's feeling better."

I wander until I find Kohl's room. I knock just in case. A shallow voice tells me to come in. There, lying shirtless in his hospital bed, lay Kohl. He had a fresh scar that ran short and sweet across his stomach.

"Maria?" he says, his voice full of hope, but he winces when he tries to sit up.

"It's okay," I tell him, urging Kohl to stay laying down.

"How are you feeling?" I ask, pulling a chair over to his bedside.

"I've been better," he admits. I try to decide if it's too fresh for me to ask, but I cannot hold myself back.

"What happened?"

"I don't know, to be completely honest. I was walking home, I was about two blocks away when I saw a few guards going the same direction as me. I decided to go a long way, going into south Genoa. I was walking when, out of nowhere, someone dragged me into an alley. They stabbed me twice in the abdomen with a rusty knife and left me there to die. Oddly enough, they didn't even bother to take my wallet. A nice man in a red suit walked past and saw me. He carried me out onto the street where people started gathering. That's about when you showed up."

I soak in all of the information as well as possible.

"I'm so sorry," I say.

"It's not your fault."

I try to believe him, but I still feel as if it's my fault we are in this situation.

We talked for a while until I rested my head on his shoulder. I must have lolled off to sleep because I awoke to a nurse telling me that visitation hours had ended. I got up off my chair and glanced at the clock. It read six-thirty p.m.

I thanked the nurse and got up to leave. As I exited the door, I heard a barely audible voice whisper, "I'll be better soon."

# 21

I smiled to myself and, in my head, whispered the plea that he'd be right. Being with Kohl gave me a steady easiness that Theo didn't grant. I made it to the front door, where I waved goodbye to Fran. I caught a taxi back to Kohl's house, praying that no guards would be present. I got my wish and I creaked open the door. I slipped off my shoes and walked into the living room. There, sitting on the couch was Theo, looking smug as ever.

"I thought you were sick," he asked with a knowing snarkiness.

"I felt better so I decided to go get some coffee," I replied.

"Did you, now?"

I narrowed my eyes at him. He must have noticed because what he did next horrified me. He pulled out my pieces of paper with all of our plans on it from underneath a magazine, and a rusty kitchen knife from his pocket.

"I know everything," he says, placing the knife on the table. "When were you going to tell me?" he asks.

I stay silent.

"Tell me, you traitor!" he shouts.

"I wasn't, okay! I couldn't kill him, okay? I am barely an assassin, okay."

"I can tell," he shouts, sending my head into a swirly pile of goo.

My brain slowly pieces things together.

"You tried to kill him, you tried to kill Kohl!" I scream.

"Yes, yes, I did. It's not like you were going to!" He takes a large breath before continuing, "And what's all this nonsense about killing the Queen? You know that would never work in a million years. Not only is that an impossible plan, but it would also be a terrible idea with a terrible outcome. What would we do without a government? Everything would collapse!"

"You are just like them," I say, my voice trembling, tears pooling in my eyes.

"Just like whom?" he says, arms crossed across his chest.

"Just like whom?" I shout. "Just like the Queen, just like all of the stuck-up snobs in the castle. What would we do without a government, you ask? We would build a new one where people aren't harvested to work free, unpaid labor for ten miserable years of their lives, that's what we would do. We would have a new king or queen who would put an end to it. Children could go to college, people would stop fearing growing up. It would be a safer world for children and adults alike. Why can't you see that, Theo? Why can't you open your eyes."

"Why can't you see that it's a foolish plan that could never work."

"Why couldn't it work?" I ask.

He didn't answer. We fought for much longer after that. Things started to get brutal. That's when he admitted everything.

"I am the one who called the Queen's guard, you know. I knew about your plan before I left for lunch. It was planned. Every. Single. Bit."

"Why were you even going through my stuff?" I yell.

"Because I knew you were hiding something."

He starts drilling into my brain, placing terrible thoughts in my head. Thoughts of murder and death. I couldn't take it anymore.

"Shut up!" I shout.

He keeps going. Rambling on about how I couldn't do a simple job. About how I was a weak assassin. About how he could do my job a hundred times better than me.

"I said, shut up!"

Before I knew it, I was flying across the room, landing on Theo, fists in the air. He didn't have time to block me before I threw my first punch.

"What are you doing, you mad woman!" he yelps.

He pushes me off and scrambles to his feet. He flees out the door. I snatch my retractable dagger off my belt loop and start chasing after him. I wasn't going to let my years of training go to waste. I'm agile on my feet and I blend into the shadows with ease. He runs past the park, heading for the woods outside of Genoa. I let him and, whenever he turned around, all he saw was the shadow of a woman pursuing him. We made it about a quarter mile into the woods, when I made my move. I sprint and speed up to tackle him. We wrestle on the ground, toppling over each other, but I never lose my grip on my knife. Eventually, I stand above him, my feet on his wrists, keeping him pinned to the ground.

"I trusted you," he whispered.

"You broke my trust the moment we entered Genoa," I say.

"What did I do wrong?"

"You made me feel like crap. You made me hate myself for not being able to kill. Maybe now I will show you the assassin I'm supposed to be."

"I'm sorry."

"Saying sorry only works on scratches. You've made a gouge."

I raised my knife above his stomach, making sure it was exactly where Kohl was stabbed.

"I loved you," he said, "I thought I was in love for the first time since Remi. I truly thought I loved you. When you kissed me, a million fireworks went off in my heart," He chuckled. A very dry, labored sound. "I was going to ask you out on a date later that week. That was silly, wasn't it?"

"Once upon a time, I thought I loved you. But that once upon a time was a long time ago. If you hadn't come with me, you may have stood a chance," I say, my face is as hard as a rock.

He looks at me, his eyes pleading to let him go.

"This shouldn't kill you," I say. "But it will hurt worse than any pain you have ever felt before. And, I swear, if I ever see your face ever again after this, I will kill you," I say, carefully drawing my dagger over his chest, and pressing down just firm enough where it doesn't break the skin.

He closes his eyes tightly, fists clenched as I lift my weapon up, and bring it down hard onto his stomach. He lets out a high-pitched agonizing scream. I pull out the weapon and look at the damage I have made. For a brief moment, my victorious smirk wavered, and I realized what I had done. It was brief, after all. I wanted him to survive, feeling the pain that he had caused Kohl. I tore off a small piece of my thin tee shirt and placed it over the wound. It soaked up the blood immediately, soaking the piece of light pink tee shirt a dark shade of burgundy.

"Good luck," I said to him, walking away, not even bothering to wipe the blood from my dagger.

## 22

I wandered back through the woods until I came upon the outskirts of town. I did a quick scan over of myself to find I did a pretty clean job. Barely a speck of blood on me, aside from the few drips on the side of my pants, where my retractable dagger is hung from a belt loop. I could pass it off easily enough if anyone mentioned it. The cool, crisp night air gave me a pleasant feel and I walked back to Kohl's house.

The front door opened with a long sigh, and I stepped inside flicking on the lights. It was a long day, but it wasn't even close to being over. I felt no remorse for what I did. I wouldn't exactly call it thrilling. That would be a terrible word to describe a terrible deed. At the most, it was a necessary act. If there is one thing that working as the Queen's assassin taught me, it's that, in a given situation where you choose between yourself and another person, you always choose yourself. I grabbed my stack of papers from the table, where they sat untouched.

I glanced over the list that I had of running ideas. I decided the best course of action would be scrapping it all. That's when the idea popped into my head. It would be extremely risky but also has the potential to be highly effective.

I jotted the idea down on a sheet of paper, making sure to box in all of the important information. Now we wait, once Kohl finally returns, we can end this all for good.

A week later, we were back in business. There was the faintest knock at the door. I stood to open it and there was Kohl, standing tall in front of me.

"Kohl!" I smiled, trying my best not to fling myself at him.

"I'm glad to be back," he said, wrapping his arms around me.

I urged him into the house and didn't know where to start.

"Why don't we sit?" I ask. "I have a lot to tell you. It's going to be a lot so I understand if it's too much, okay? Just let me know if you need a break."

He takes a deep breath, wincing slightly.

Before I start, I look at him. I study him hard, making sure each individual inch of him is there.

"Is it bad?" I ask, not unlocking my eyes from his.

He glances away, stealing a look at his stomach.

"It's not too bad," he promises, lifting his shirt up.

There was a rigid four-inch scar tracing over his stomach. The scar was raised and still looks incredibly fresh.

He ran his fingers over the scar and, without looking at me, said, "Thank you for visiting. You're the only one who bothered. Exccept the press, of course. But I refused to answer any questions."

"I couldn't imagine not coming to see you," I say.

He smiles at me, a sad sight compared to his usual bright grin.

Kohl cleared his throat before asking me to continue.

"Okay, to start, I may or may not have done something I regret. I found out who tried to kill you. It… was Theo. And, well, when I found out, I freaked. I chased him out into the woods and gave him a taste of his own medicine." I looked away, too scared to see the look on Kohl's face.

He didn't say anything for a while, but then he scooted closer to me. I still couldn't bear to look at him.

"It's okay. I suspected as much. Something about him always made me uneasy."

"I still did something unnecessary," I argued.

He stopped to think a minute before saying, "You did what you thought had to be done. Your judgment is better than anyone else's here," he tried to assure me and, while his voice was the most sincere I had heard in a while, part of me still couldn't believe him.

When I still couldn't meet his gaze, he gently grabbed my chin and turned it to look at him.

"I don't regret anything I did," I said softly. "If that makes a difference."

"I want you to be confident in yourself and your decisions."

" I can try," I mumbled.

"Why don't you tell me the rest," he said, staring intently at me while I spoke.

"Well, now that Theo isn't here, we have nothing that we have to hide. I was thinking about sending a letter to Jackie. If we could get her to rally some rebel soldiers we could attack. They would never see it coming until it was too late."

"Smart," he replied. "We better start writing."

# 23

We started writing our letter almost immediately, starting our letter off strong.

"Dear Jackie,

We hope this letter finds you well. We are writing to propose a plan that we believe could greatly change the outcome of the current battle. We know that this is a risky request, but we are willing to take the chance in the hopes of making a positive impact.

We were wondering if you would be willing to speak with some of the guards and, potentially, even some of the people in the biology department in order to gather support for our cause. We understand that this may be a difficult task, as these individuals may not agree, which is why it would be smartest to target those you know aren't as loyal to the Queen. However, we believe that, with your help, we may be able to sway some of the more loyal people to our side and utilize their skills and knowledge to our advantage.

We understand that this is a bold request and we do not take it lightly. We also understand that it may put you in a dangerous position. However, we believe that the potential benefits of this plan far outweigh the risks. If you are willing to take this chance with us, we would be greatly appreciative of your support.

Sincerely, Maria and Kohl"

After we finished writing the letter, I sealed it up and brought it to the post office to send it off. Kohl let out a sigh as we left the office. "Now we wait," he said.

I turned to him and asked, "What can we do in the meantime?"

He thought for a moment before responding. "Well, we could always study battle strategy. I'm sure if we go to the library, we can find plenty of books on the castle and how it has been used in past battles. It might be helpful to know our enemy's tactics and strengths, as well as come up with our own plans for victory.

I nodded in agreement. "That's a good idea. Time to make some real progress. We can't accept anything but a win."

With that, we set off toward the library, determined to learn as much as we could about the upcoming battle. We knew that every little bit of knowledge could be the key to our success.

As I approached the library, I was immediately struck by its grandeur. The building was adorned with intricate pieces of architecture, such as domed roofs and terracotta walls that seemed to glow in the sunlight. The exterior was further enhanced by rows of large windows that let in an abundance of natural light. I couldn't wait to see what the inside had in store.

Upon entering the library, I felt as though I had been transported to another world. The floor was made of sprawling marble, and there were rows upon rows of shelves filled with books as far as the eye could see. The walls were curved and painted a light, airy color, and the furniture was a combination of dark mahogany and brown leather.

As Kohl and I walked further into the library, we approached a woman sitting behind a desk. I asked her if she could direct us to the section with history books. She smiled and silently led us to a set of shelves that were double-sided and packed with books on the subject. Kohl then asked if she could show us the section where the history of the castle was kept. The woman nodded and led us to the fourth shelf, where we found an entire section dedicated to the topic.

"Thank you so much," I said, grinning at the woman. She returned my smile and made her way back to her desk.

"Let's split up," I suggested to Kohl. "We can both take a stack of books and look through them. We may be here for a while."

"Good idea, Maria," Kohl replied.

I started by grabbing three books. One was titled, "The History of Castle Marion." Another was called, "Behind the Scenes: Royal Castle," and the final was, "Castle Marion: The Truth." All of them had an ominous feel to them, which is why I picked them. I hope these books will help me uncover some ways to help kill the Queen. All information is crucial. I started with the one on the history of the castle. I skimmed through the book, finding mostly unimportant information. There were a few pictures that stood out to me, such as pictures of old rooms, and the way the artillery was positioned at guard towers. I took pictures on Kohl's phone. There was one line that stuck out in the whole book, though. "Some say that the castle may even be a break-in proof." Maybe that was just there to deter any possible intruders but I still jotted it down anyway. Next, I grabbed Behind the Scenes: Royal Castle, setting the other book aside on the edge of the sprawling mahogany table. This book created a very different tone from the other one, more light-hearted, as it was describing a behind-the-scenes blooper for a movie. It did have some very useful information though. It had information on the fourth-generation king. King Ruthford III. A strong leader, but not the one who started this whole mess. I read further into the book, becoming absorbed in its contents. I found out the first King of Avion was King Ruthford I. He started this program because he and his wife wanted people working for them, so they didn't have to spend more resources on the information. Quite a stupid reason, if you ask me. I added that book to the pile I had started, grabbing the last one. This one held the most information out of them all. It gave the backstory of the castle and, most important, the secret passages connecting the rooms.

"Bingo," I whispered under my breath, soaking in all the information. This would work perfectly to help assassinate the Queen.

## 24

I called out to Kohl, who was intently bent over a thick, leather-bound volume. "Find anything good?". He looked up at me with a concentrated expression, his brows furrowed in thought.

"Yeah, I think I've stumbled upon something that could give us an edge. How about you? Uncover any useful information?"

I scanned the pages of my own book, searching for valuable insights that I knew were there. Finally, I nodded and replied, "Yes, I've found some promising leads as well. Why don't we regroup and share our findings?" Kohl walked over and placed his books on the table. They were beautifully crafted hardcover editions, with intricate designs etched into the covers—one was a deep, matte green and the other a rich crimson red.

I opened my book to the section containing a map of all the secret passages. Kohl gasped in amazement as he laid eyes on it. "This is incredible," he exclaimed. "Maybe we do stand a chance of overthrowing the Queen after all."

I grinned at him and asked, "What about you? What valuable information did you discover?"

Kohl flipped to a page in the emerald green book, treating the old, delicate pages with reverence. On it was the layout of the castle before it underwent reconstruction. The drawing was incredibly detailed, showing all of the small, intricate details such as doorways, and how all of the halls connected into one large room. I recognized this room as the Great Hall. The drawing didn't quite capture the grandeur of the high, arched walls or the opulent furniture, but it effectively conveyed the essence of the space. Underneath the image was the caption, "While this was the layout for the olden castle, some people believe that they just renovated the castle. It's possible that the castle still has this layout, but it would be difficult to ascertain without looking at it from above with the roof removed."

"This is fantastic," I exclaimed, trying not to let my excitement get the better of me. "Now we have the potential layouts of the castle and secret passageways!"

Kohl had a sly look on his face as he turned to the burgundy book. He flipped to the very last page of the book, revealing some sort of code. "This," he said, "is the key to disarming any booby traps we might encounter in the secret passages. I'd assume they would be inactive now, but it's better to be safe than sorry."

My smile stretched even wider, spreading from ear to ear. I threw myself at him, forgetting that he had just recently recovered from his injuries.

"I'm sorry," I said quickly, realizing that I may have squeezed him too tightly.

"No, you're fine," he replied, his determination shining in his eyes. "I won't let an injury get in the way of our ultimate goal. We will assassinate the Queen if it is the last thing we do."

"Why don't we go check these books out of the library? We should study them and make sure we know them well," I say.

"Good idea," Kohl replies.

We head to the counter and check out the three books we selected.

We took our time walking home, enjoying the longer, more scenic route that we had chosen. The almost Orca air smelled sweet and fresh, Orca was my favorite month, filled with warm air and enjoyable outdoor activites, and I wished that we could wander the city for hours. However, time was not on our side, so we eventually made our way to Kohl's house. As we approached the house, we stopped in our tracks when we saw the mess that had occurred. The door handle was twisted and mangled as if someone had tried with all their might to break in but failed. The window in the front was also smashed, the sharp edges lightly stained with blood.

"What happened?" I whispered under my breath. Kohl looked terrified and didn't say a word, just held his books tightly to his chest. When he didn't make any effort to move, I reached into his pocket and retrieved the keys. My hands were shaking as I managed to get the key into the lock and open the door.

Inside, the house wasn't a mess. I was expecting nothing left on the polished hardwoods or clean walls. It wasn't ransacked at all. We searched around the house, looking for a trace of any human being. Nothing was found. That was until I saw an envelope resting prominently on the kitchen counter. It hadn't been there before we had left, and I examined it carefully. It was a cream-colored envelope sealed with blue wax. That was odd. Until I turned it over and saw the words: To, Maria. Love, Theo.

# 25

My hands trembled as I picked up the letter and spun it around. The envelope was staring at me menacingly, not revealing its true intentions.

"Kohl," I shout, it was barely a shout, actually. More like a whimper. He walks over, his back slouched and worry sinking into his eyes.

I don't say anything. I just show him the letter asking the silent question: Should I open it? He nods but slightly looks away as I tear away the blue seal, a color I didn't realize had significance until I read the letter inside.

I held the cream parchment in my hand, feeling rough, yet smooth, feel in my hands. I read every word carefully, making sure I knew exactly what I was reading.

"Dear Maria,

I would simply like to say thank you. Thank you for all the suffering you put me through. You couldn't kill the man, could you? I hope that stab kills Kohl and takes you along with him. I thought we were friends, but I refuse to get all sentimental about the "old times". I just wanted you to know that the Queen knows your plans. Every. Single. One.

"You might as well give up before you get ahead of yourself. I bet Kohl regrets ever helping you. You ruined his life, you know. I also thought it would be nice of me to tell you that I have been appointed as the Queen's new assassin. Now, it's time to get to the good part. In case you couldn't tell by that lovely, navy blue seal, the Queen is declaring war against you if you don't stand down. If you're going down, might as well go down a fighter, eh? I bet that is what you are thinking. Well, I just want to let you know one thing: You and Kohl against an army of thousands don't stand a chance. See, Maria, this is why you should never show mercy. It always comes back to haunt you. I'll see you on the battlefield.

Your 'best friend',

Theo"

I clenched my fingers tighter around the letter, on the verge of tearing it to pieces. I couldn't help but feel a sense of betrayal as I read the line, "Your 'best friend'." I knew he was being sarcastic, but a true friend would have listened to me and considered my ideas before moving forward.

Kohl placed a comforting hand on my shoulder, sensing my distress. He didn't need to say anything, his presence alone was enough to ease my mind.

"What do we do now?" Kohl asked after a moment of silence.

"We do what we've always planned to do," I replied, glancing down at the letter. "We kill the Queen."

The next few days passed in a blur of preparations. We spent our days practicing, studying, and strategizing. We had a clear understanding of the Queen's castle, including the traps and guard positions. We received a letter from Jackie that confirmed our plans and provided details on when and where to meet her soldiers.

"Jackie will have around fifty soldiers ready at the outskirts of town on the ninth of this month," I recited from the letter, showing Kohl a map that Jackie had included. "She doesn't think the Queen suspects anything, but it's better to take a more discreet approach. Look at this map she drew, it shows us the best way to enter the city."

Kohl studied the map carefully, tracing a path from a hidden gate in the woods to a secret stretch of land that I hadn't even known existed.

I continued summarizing the letter. "Jackie also wanted to remind us that the Queen's army will be much larger than our own. And Theo has taken over my job, as we already know."

Kohl nodded along with every word I said, his expression growing increasingly somber. "So, this is happening on Saturday. That only gives us four more days." He glanced around the room as if he expected to find someone hiding in the shadows. "I just want to know what happens next. When she's gone, what will happen? She has no children and no spouse. All this time, we've been assuming that something good will come of this, but what if we get arrested or put on trial for murder? What if we spend the rest of our lives rotting away in a cell?"

Kohl's eyes met mine, and I could see the fear and uncertainty in them. "At least we'll have each other,""I tried to offer a reassuring smile. "Even if we end up in a cell."

He began pacing back and forth in front of me, his movements growing more agitated with each step. "We need to prepare, Maria. It'" not enough," Kohl said, determination creeping back into his voice. "We need to be ready for anything."

## 26

I stared at the blank wall next to my bed, eyes glued open. I was unable to sleep, the nerves were too much. I have been tossing and turning all night. Slowly, I sat up and wrapped myself in a cocoon of blankets before standing and making my way to Kohl's room. I knocked faintly on the door. A shallow voice inside beckoned me in. The door creaked open, and there was Kohl laying on his bed.

"Can't sleep?" he asks as I waddle in and settle on the edge of his bed.

"No," I reply. "I take it you can't either?"

He shakes his head in response.

"Are you ready?" I ask. "Our lives change tomorrow. For better or for worse."

He stares at the ceiling, not replying. I gently nudge him until he looks at me.

"Not really," he says.

I lay down next to him, my blanket cocoon keeping me warm as the room around me becomes increasingly cold.

"We are going to assassinate the Queen," he breathes into my ear.

"Yes," I say. "Yes, we are."

Before we know it, the morning light is bright on the horizon. I lay awake next to Kohl, I hadn't slept the whole night but, after a while, he had fallen into a deep sleep.

I shook him awake, his groggy eyes meeting mine before he sat up and yawned. Soon after that, we were running frantically around the halls of the house, taking time to collect everything we needed. I quickly put on my black leather pants, they were slightly loose and I prayed they wouldn't fall down. I pulled the tan and black leather bodice over my head. I smoothed out the corset-like bodice, admiring the tan stripes running down the sides of it. This was the official Queen's assassin uniform. Might as well give her the terror that she gave hundreds of others when they saw a person approaching them in this outfit, weapon drawn. I glanced in the mirror, pulling my hair into a bun to keep the stray whisps out of my face. Soon enough, Kohl was ready to go, his jeans and baggy grey tee shirt making him the most notable assassin ever.

I headed over to my room, shoving as many weapons as possible into the deep pockets of my cargo pants. Once I had an assortment of switchblades in my pocket, four daggers on my belt loops, and a holstered pistol, I told Kohl I was ready to go.

It would be a long walk to our destination, and we were sure to attract unwanted attention. As we wandered down the street that led to the castle, we got several stares, some scared, others unreadable. Once we arrived at the edge of the shack that had first started our mission, we noticed several things that seemed off. All of the men who were usually lugging materials around and loading them into piles were gone. The shack was boarded up. We cautiously walked around the edge of the building following the directions on our map. We came upon a hedge bush around three hundred feet from where the shack was. There, hidden in the shrubs, was a black, slightly rusted gate. The chain that used to hold it shut was on the ground, and the padlock busted open. That must have been Jackie's doing. Now was the long part. We had to walk about a mile to get to the clearing that framed the back of the castle. The early air was hot, sticking to me and making the leather bodice all the more uncomfortable.

When we saw the edges of one of the peaked roofs faintly in the distance, poking out at us from the edge of the hill we were standing on, we started walking even faster. When we were finally done stumbling down the hill, we were in front of a sprawling field. It was quite beautiful, aside from the army of people that were standing before us. It was, by no means, as large as the Queens, maybe around a quarter of their army. But it was still something and I couldn't keep the smile off my face. Jackie was standing tall before them, her wife standing proudly beside her.

"Maria, you're here!" Jackie cried, putting her hands on my shoulders and studying me carefully.

"I was able to round up more people than expected. I think there are around a hundred. Some soldiers, some townsfolk. I hope this will do," she said.

I looked out into the vast sea of people. This is so much more real now that I am actually here, standing before them.

"This is wonderful, Jackie," I say, unable to contain the smile on my lips.

We are still a ways away from the castle, but we can see it in the distance. It won't be far.

Kohl and I wandered through the sea of people, the sound of people wishing us a good battle echoing around us.

I couldn't have been more ready as I got to the end of the sea, and began to shout, "On this day, we take back our home! We are ready to fight for what is right. This will be a historical moment!" I smiled as the waves of encouraging shouts began to wash over us. But then Kohl glanced around, waiting for everyone to finish.

"Everyone's attention please!" he yelled, his dark, rich voice stretching out over the crowd. Once everyone had quieted down, Kohl announced, "We feel the need to point out that anyone involved could suffer consequences. We don't know what will happen if we fail our mission. It will not be good. So, before we begin, I would like to encourage everyone to think it over. Are you sure this is what you want?""

The second of silence stretched into a minute before someone shouted out, "They can't kill us all! They can't lock us all up!"

Shouts of other people agreeing were scattered around the crowd. Not one person backed down. Not one person out of this whole army. I smiled at Kohl, and he returned it with an ear-to-ear grin of his own.

"It's time," I whispered to him under my breath.

"Yes, It is," he breathed in.

I took his hand in mine, tangling our fingers together. We glanced at each other once more before triumphantly raising our hands high.

"It is time to fight back!" I roared over the sea of people.

Their rallying cries rang out over the meadow, the light breeze carrying on the message to anyone willing to help.

# 27

We lowered our arms, feeling the seconds tick by. It was almost time to start the trek, and I still had a lot of instructions to give.

"Everyone listen up!" I screamed, my voice booming over the army before me.

Almost instantly, they quieted down.

"Everyone get in a line. We will separate you into groups." Soon enough, a long line was formed, twisting and turning through the open stretch of land.

Although I thought the sorting was going to last forever, it went by quicker than I expected. We quickly sorted several men and women into their groups. Once everyone was where they were supposed to be, I addressed them again.

"You are group A," I announced, pointing to the group to my right. "Your job will be to guard the outside of the castle. No one goes in and no one goes out, got it? If anyone tries to leave, try not to hurt them unless it is necessary. Children are the only exception. I don't think there should be any children, but it's better to go over it and not need it than to need it and not know what to do."

I watched for several head nods before continuing.

"You, are group B,""I said, pointing to the group on my left. "You will be the battle group. I have very specific orders for you though, so make sure you are listening carefully. You are to only kill those who attack you first, understand? If someone is willing to stand down, allow them that option. Whether we like these people or not, they are still human beings. However, if they choose to continue fighting, feel free to use any means necessary. Your safety is always important, as well. If you decide this may not be the best option for you once we are on the battlefield, there is no pressure to stay." I whipped my head over to group A. "If anyone in group B needs to leave, you are to let them, understood? Part of these rules also applies to you. If you feel the need to leave, you may. If you are attacked, fight back. For so many years we have lost the battle, but we are finally ready to win the war! Do we have any questions before we break?"

I waited for anyone to raise their hands, but the only thing that followed my question with silence.

"Anything to add?" I asked Kohl.

He nodded his head yes and said, "Just try your best. We have one goal, and one goal only. Kill the Queen, and that is it."

Everyone in the crowd's eyes gleamed with excitement as I barked one final time, "Okay, so we are all good on our strategy. Jackie will lead group A and I will lead B. Good luck, soldiers. You don't know how much this will affect future children. We are doing this for the greater good." There was one final cheer as we led our groups away.

Kohl and I walked briskly, our large group easily keeping up with our long stride.

Soon enough, we were approaching the castle, the very one that got us into this mess in the first place. We crept along the side of the beautiful architecture. I placed my hand on the rough gray stone, running my fingers in the grooves as we slowly crept along the side.

"This is it," I whispered to Kohl as we came upon a hatch nestled in the tall grass along the side of the castle. It was lined by brick and barely visible unless you were looking for it. My fingers brushed the rim of the hatch, looking for a release to get in. My fingers latched onto a spot that felt promising. I lifted it up carefully and peered into the dark hole below.

"Everyone goes in now, we will follow," Kohl announced.

Everyone started pouring into the hatch, climbing down the ladder at a considerable speed.

"Ready?" Kohl asked, grabbing my hand. I squeezed it letting him know that I was, but didn't follow him down immediately.

"I will be down quickly, I am just going to do one more quick scan to make sure no one followed," I told him.

He nodded. "Be safe, If you aren't down in a couple of minutes, I'm coming back up to check on you."

"I'll be quick," I promised, offering a reassuring smile. He reluctantly finished climbing down into the darkness.

I glanced around the area again, quickly doing a check by looking around the edges of the castle and scanning any bushes or trees for anyone lurking in the shadows.

I lowered my body into the hole and, just as I was about to close the hatch, I heard the very first gunshot. The war had begun.

# 28

The inside of the tunnel I was dropped into was small, dark, and damp.

"Everyone in a straight line!" I ordered, waiting for the several bodies to be pushed up against the wall before I could walk to the front of the line.

"In this part, you have to be very careful and listen well. We will come out of this tunnel in the Great Hall, around the middle of the castle. There is a possibility of traps, so make sure you watch your step.""They nodded, acknowledging my tip. We slowly delved deeper into the tunnels, all light beginning to fade away.

"Does anyone have anything to start a fire?" I call down the line of people.

One man steps out of the line, slowly making his way to me as he hands me a worn-out box of matches.

"Thank you," I say to him. I walk over to the wall where a dusty old torch lies mounted on the wall. I hold the box of matches with my mouth as I use both hands to rip the torch off of the wall.

"Can you hold this?" I asked Kohl, handing him the torch.

He nods and I grab a match out of the box, flicking it quickly on the side until a flame starts dancing across the tip of the match. Slowly, I lower it into the torch, and it quickly catches fire from all of the dust and debris. Kohl hands me the torch and we continue down the hallway.

As we were walking, I felt as if we were almost getting too lucky. There is no way that there weren't any remaining traps.

And I was right. We soon came upon a tall, arched doorway. A thin tripwire lay already broken before it, indicating that someone had already tried to get in this way before. Inside the doorway, which appeared to stretch around six feet, were axes, the blades somewhat shiny, and traced with dried blood. They were also swinging back and forth in one, fast, smooth motion. There were deep gasps around the small hallway, and I could tell some people were finally beginning to get nervous.

"It's okay, everyone. We know how to handle this," Kohl assured them. Our tiny army slowly started to calm down.

I got on my hands and knees and started to push the dirt and old debris around, looking for any sign of a lever, button, or pressure plate. The book wasn't super clear on what to look for in this situation. Kohl and I scoured the floor, running our fingers through unknown substances. That is, until I found it, a small, very hidden, stone button. It blended in perfectly with the floor and was hidden in the crevice where two walls meet at the corner of the doorway.

"I found it!" I called to Kohl.

I was just about to press the button when Kohl cried out, "Wait! Everyone, duck."

The group frantically dropped down to their knees just as my fingers made contact with the button. Not even a second later, the axes stopped, but hundreds of arrows poured from hidden compartments in the walls. Once they were scattered across the floor, I stood up carefully, looking at the compartments mindfully before okaying the rest of the group to stand. Some people looked a little shaky on their feet, but others looked fired up at the experience. It appeared it made them even more ready to fight. We proceeded through the doorway, pushing aside random bones of, what I assumed were, past intruders.

It was a rather long walk until we saw the rotting spiral staircase leading up to the great hall.

"Okay, everyone, listen up," I announced.

"When we go up there, be ready for anything. We don't know how many guards there will be, and we don't know what part of the hall we will come out in. Just follow Kohl and me and be as quiet as you can."

Everyone nodded, silently awaiting their next command.

I slowly started to climb the staircase, the familiar feeling making my heart ache. I reached the top and, ever so carefully, opened the door, silently.

We came out into a scene I wasn't quite expecting. About half of group A were battling it out in the long, grand hall. The other half was struggling but still succeeding to keep people at bay from entering the castle.

It was time. My army knew what to do, so I leaped into action and drew my dagger.

The real fight had finally begun.

# 29

I stood face to face with a man who wore a shocked expression. He gasped my name, "Maria?" while ducking under incoming attacks from all around us. My dagger was drawn, ready for a fight, but I held back. I didn't know who he was but, if he was willing to stand down and wait with group A at the gates, or even fight with us, I wouldn't have to kill him. "I-I can't believe it! I thought you were on our side?" he muttered.

I looked him up and down, studying his armor and weapons, before replying, "I am on the side that doesn't kill people for not being good at something. That's what got us here in the first place, correct?" He glances around the room at the ongoing fight and the blood staining the once-elegant marble floors. The sound of clashing swords and the cries of the wounded filled the air. "Do you wish to stand down?" I asked, my voice steady and firm. He looked at me, at all of our surroundings once more before his face hardened.

"No. I won't be a traitor. She may not be right, but I don't think she should die either."

"So be it, then," I replied, readying myself for the fight. In an instant, I was on top of him, dagger pressed to his chest. A moment of guilt surfaced, the same feeling I had after I had assaulted Theo. But it didn't last long. Just as I was about to finish the deed, he jumped up, in a flash, back on his feet, his steel dagger displayed promptly in front of him. He went in for a swipe, but I easily avoided it. As the man stumbled over his own feet, I took a short time to spring behind him. I quickly wrapped my arm around his torso, before stabbing him squarely in the back. His body dropped, limp, to the floor. I looked at the blood that was splattered on my hands and once more felt a ping of guilt. But giving a quick glance around the room, seeing my injured or diseased allies and enemies, I knew it was too late for guilt. I had to push on and fight for my cause.

I pushed through the throngs of people, my heart pounding in my chest. The castle was in chaos, with guards and royal officials fighting desperately to maintain control. Every time I stepped over a body or had to resist the urge to help an injured ally, I would close my eyes and push forward. Kohl was always slightly behind me, fighting alongside me and helping me battle through the ranks. My dagger was slick with blood and sweat by the time we reached the door I needed to get to. We had managed to escape to a part of the castle where no one else had yet arrived. I was just a few steps away from the door where the Queen lay, but I didn't know what to do or what to feel. Just as I was about to place my hand on the cold iron handle, I felt the tip of a very sharp, cold sword pressed against my back.

"Don't move," a dark, all-too-familiar voice advised.

"Theo," I growled, my teeth gritting together.

"I am glad to see you too, Maria," he replied.

I could feel the determination in Theo's eyes, like daggers glaring into my soul, and I knew that he wouldn't hesitate to kill me if I made the wrong move. He was my old friend, but we were now on opposite sides of the battle.

"Turn around slowly," he commanded, lifting the long, silver blade of his weapon just enough for me to turn around and face him.

Almost instantly, I was scanning the room for Kohl. He sat on the floor, thrown against a wall. His arms and legs had been bound with a thick tan rope, and a cloth gag was shoved around his mouth. I clenched my fist, not being able to stand seeing the state he was in.

"So, I see you went through with it," Theo tsked, pacing shortly back in forth in front of me, his sword still drawn, but no longer pointed at me.

"And I see that you still haven't opened your eyes," I countered, reaching for the pistol holstered on my waist, knowing it would be far too dangerous to bend down for the dagger resting a few feet away from Theo.

He paused for a moment at that remark, opening his mouth and then closing it, clenching his jaw tightly.

"What is it? Why did you choose to fight against me? I don't care if you say it's a lost cause, at least it is right."

"Is it right?" Theo retorted. "You will leave hundreds of thousands of people without a government. Without guidance. Is that what you really want?"

I looked down the hall at the few one-on-one battles that were slowly creeping up the hallways.

"I can figure that out later," I admitted. "But why do you choose to stay? You have experienced the cruelty of the Queen first-hand."

He thought on that for a minute before responding, "Well, I couldn't give you a fair answer, to be honest. My reason, my motive is the fact that we need a leader. It may not be fair, but that applies to everything, does it not? Life isn't fair."

"She kills innocent people!" I cry.

"I can't argue that it's not wrong," he admitted. "But the people who survive still get a chance at life."

"Wouldn't you want revenge? For Remi?"

Theo's face hardens at her name, softening for only a brief moment.

"Don't bring up her name."

"It would make sense for you to be on my side, fight for her."

"Please don't talk about her anymore."

I don't press.

"I will give you one more chance at redemption, Maria," Theo says with an unreadable face.

I don't even think before saying,

"I would never even consider it."

## 30

"So be it then," he said.

I drew my pistol in one quick motion, but Theo was quicker than I was, and he had me cornered against the wall. He was able to disarm me, his knee up against my stomach and one hand tearing the gun out of my hand. My pistol clattered to the floor and slid about six feet away from me. The gears in my head turned at lightning speed, rushing over the several bits and pieces of my former training.

Always be behind the target.

Don't let them disarm you.

Don't let them within five feet unless you are ready to attack.

So far, I had failed at all of those rules, that was until another one appeared in my brain.

If you are cornered, disarmed, or in a dangerous situation, the best way to get them off is to push on one of several pressure points that can harm or paralyze someone, including their groin, eyes, or kneecaps. If you are at a closer distance, the temples can also work.

Taking account of the position I was in, I glanced Theo up and down. It was as if everything was in slow motion. The way that he brought down his weapon above my head, the way Kohl howled through his gag, and how, at just the right time in one continuous motion, I was able to escape. Just before the sword met contact with my skull, I reached out and tried to punch Theo in his eye, but I missed. Thankfully, when I'd kneed him just underneath his left kneecap, I was spot on. Theo stumbled back, yelping in pain as I slid across the floor and grabbed my pistol. Theo stood there paralyzed for a moment, just as I loaded the gun and took a shot, aiming directly at his heart. But, because of the way my hands were uncontrollably shaking, I missed the shot. The bullet grazed the side of his shirt, ripping the fabric and giving him a cut on his side. The scar that I had given him was on display, and I thought I would feel guilty, but I was wrong. Just as I was reloading my gun, he was able to move quickly, grabbing a knife and throwing it at me. I tried to dodge it, but it landed on my shoulder. I hissed with pain before taking two large steps in front of me, getting closer to Theo as I squinted with one eye, aiming for his chest once more. This time, I didn't miss it. A flashback of the same gunshot arose through my mind, but I ignored it as I watched Theo's lifeless body drop to the floor, and the sound of his sword clattering to the ground.

I stood there for a second, paralyzed myself. I was staring at Theo's lifeless body on the floor, the way the blood poured out of his chest and pooled around him.

"He could have made a different choice," I reminded myself. "He brought this on himself."

I looked over at my shoulder; a knife with a brown leather handle protruding out of my arm. I knew better than to pull it out until I had something to wrap it with, so I left it there, the warm sticky blood merely trickling down my arm.

I made my way over to Kohl in a blink of an eye, removing his gag first. He took a deep breath as I used one of my smaller knives to cut through his binds.

"You're hurt," he gasped, taking in all of the air that he could.

"I'm fine," I assured him, even though it was clear I wasn't.

"Sit down," he told me, pointing to the empty space in front of him.

"We don't have time," I urged, glancing frantically around the room.

"You can't fight with one arm," he argued.

Reluctantly, I sat in front of him on the mucky, blood-stained floor.

"This is going to hurt," he warned just before he slowly pulled the knife from my arm.

I ground my teeth in pain, and let out an agonizing yell. Almost as soon as the knife was out, the blood started pouring from the wound.

"Take a deep breath," he advised me. He tightly wrapped his former gag around my arm. It was thin, and it soaked through very quickly.

He tore off a piece of his tee shirt, leaving the side of his muscular torso exposed. He tied that around my arm as well, and it didn't soak through all the way, mostly splotches.

"That's as good as it will get," he sighed, standing up.

He offered out his hand, and I took it, pulling myself up with my good arm.

Kohl walked over to Theo's pale body, all of his blood drained out of him.

"It"s a shame," Kohl said, his voice full of genuine sorrow.

"It is," I agreed. "You'd think he would have wanted to fight on our side, for his past lover, Remi. She suffered firsthand by the Queen. But... I think that Theo was a coward. He was too scared to take the action that needed to be done."

Kohl looked at me before wrapping me in a tight hug, carefully avoiding my shoulder. I returned it, placing my head in the crook of his neck. We stayed like that for only a brief moment, taking a silent moment to acknowledge our feelings, before we untangled ourselves.

I took a deep breath before looking at Kohl and grabbing his hand. We walked over to Theo's body and crouched down beside him. I reached into his pocket, unable to look at his gaping eyes, and I pulled out a large iron key. I then walked over to the door, and my hand shook as I placed the key into the keyhole.

The door opened with a creak, into a dark, familiar room. The dark throne was standing tall, staring down at me. The room was dark aside from the natural sunlight shining through the windows. And I noticed one thing about the room. It was empty.

# 31

"It can't be," Kohl gasped, entering the vacant room. Not a sign of life was present. Everything was left the same way since I left.

Determined to find answers, I began searching through the piles of books on her shelves, examining each one for clues. I even approached her throne, placing my hands in between the crevices of the cushion in search of any hints. But my efforts were in vain, and I was left feeling even more confused and lost.

"I'm going to go outside and check the courtyard," I said, taking long strides toward the door.

"Wait!" Kohl called out, hurrying to catch up to me. "We have to stick together," he reminded me.

I smiled and nodded. "Of course."

We stepped out of the door and into the beautiful garden that I had walked through on my previous visit. In the light of day, the garden had lost its mysterious feel and the creatures of the night had been replaced by more vibrant ones. Although I didn't relish the idea of being back in the castle, I couldn't help but feel a sense of nostalgia for the peacefulness of the garden. But this peace was quickly broken by a feeling of unease that was creeping up on me. The garden was too quiet, and the unanswered questions were making me feel increasingly anxious. That's when I heard it. A rustle in the leaves, barely even audible, but my keen ears were able to pick up on it.

My head quickly shot over to the lingiaon berry bush—a rare but delicious purple fruit. Kohl's head moved in harmony with mine, as we watched a sleek, shadowy figure move from bush to bush, too fast to be seen, but not heard. Then a growl started to emit from the residing spot the creature chose. It was as if a chorus of grumbling started to play, as one of the creatures stepped out into the daylight. I knew the creature as a former friend, my best friend, from my time at the castle. His name was Lupu, he was a large black wolf, with eyes as dark as night, and a long, fluffy tail. His mouth was pulled back into a snarl, exposing his white, sharp teeth. His brother, Manjin, wasn't far behind. Manjin was slightly taller than Lupu, standing at almost four-and-a-half feet tall and nearly six feet long. Manjin was more graceful than his brother, with sleek gray fur that fans out around his face, making him look more like a mythical creature rather than a dentrin, meaning a large wolf in the ancient tongue. Manjin's teeth were bared, but he wasn't trying to circle me, he was standing still, examining me. Whenever I moved, he inched closer.

I tried to remember the commands, maybe to see if they would still follow them.

"Bok youn!" I shouted to them, trying to see if they would back away.

They didn't budge.

I shouted other various commands at them, but I barely got a reaction.

I was starting to give up when I heard a slow clap float through the garden followed by a laugh. A dark silhouette stepped out from the trees, shouting, "Retriveo!"

Both Manjin and Lupu stepped down, running happily to this mysterious person.

"Good boys!" their voice cooed, petting the wolves behind their ears. They both whined in delight.

My eyes widened as I began to comprehend the commands the dogs were given.

There is only one other person who would know those commands and my theory was proven right as they stepped into a beam of light. The golden light highlighted the loose tendrils of hair that framed her face and made the color in her eyes pop even more. My heart began to race when she saw my face.

"Maria," she grinned, nothing sincere on her face. "Welcome home."

## 32

I tried not to grind my teeth as I answered as sarcastically as possible, "Your Majesty. So great to finally see you."

She stepped closer, Lupu and Manjin at her heels, awaiting any commands. Manjin even approached me, sniffing me curiously before trotting back to Aria.

Stepping closer, now only feet away from me, she said with a sort of growl, "Where did your trip go wrong? You seemed loyal enough before. But who's this next to you now? Kohl, is it? Step forward, my boy. Let me look at you."

Kohl looked at me, but I didn't say a word. It was also up to him to determine the outcome of this battle.

Slowly, he moved one foot forward, then another until he stopped in front of the Queen. Looking at the ground, Aria said, "Oh, dear, you do look so much like your father," she sighed, taking a finger and tipping his chin upward so he was looking her in the eyes.

"How is the old fellow? Is he holding up nicely?" Kohl winced at her touch and, when he didn't answer the question, she pushed him backward. He stumbled back, landing on me, where I caught him and steadied him once more.

"I suppose you found out my true intent, yes? Well, I would say I owe you an explanation but, in this case, I feel that is not needed. But, Maria, my dear, I feel you owe me an excuse of some sort. Why did you switch sides? Why did you betray me?" Her voice was cold and, when she spoke, it was as if the ground trembled.

I began to sweat even more as I spoke, but my voice did not break. "I think you know the answer to that. I have never been one to do the wrong thing. All of those people I have killed for you, all of the families that I have broken. I can barely forgive myself now. I have stripped several children from their fathers, wives from their husbands, and children from their parents. I won't do it anymore. The only reason I took this job was so that I could be free from all of this," I say, motioning to the garden around me. "Not only did I find out the person I was supposed to murder was one of the only significant people in my life throughout my childhood, and I knew I wouldn't be able to do such a task. Especially when I found out he did nothing wrong."

I braced for her response, but she just stared at me with a hard-to-read expression on her face for a minute before opening her mouth and then closing it. She stopped pacing, looking at me with a smirk, before saying,

"Well, isn't that heart-touching; long-lost lovers brought together in the worst of circumstances," she scowled as she continued, "You could have lived in the lap of luxury all your life, you know that, right? You could have looked the other way. Now, look what you've done.

You killed Theo which was a surprise. I thought you had something going on. He was innocent enough, right? You have already done so many terrible things, what's one more? Face it, Maria. You are just like me."

Kohl stepped closer to me, and I could almost see his body shaking with fear, or maybe it was anger.

"Don't worry," I whispered to him. "She's bluffing. She's not so scary." His body relaxed with that remark and he slowly started to calm down. I was about to reply to the Queen's remark when I was caught off guard. Kohl started speaking for me.

"There is a difference between bad and evil. Do you at least know that much?" he scolded. Kohl suddenly looked taller, with broader shoulders and a deeper voice. Less like the clumsy teenager my brain still thought he was, and more like an adult. Aria wrinkled her delicate nose at him, not making a peep. Manjin and Lupu must have felt Kohl's shift in dominance, as Lupu's ears sat up taller on his fluffy black head, and Manjin looked a little warier at his possible opponent.

"The difference between the two is that all people do bad things, we are all human and they happen even if we didn't mean for them to. Evil people do things to hurt others for the joy of it, the rush they feel, and they don't think anything of the consequences A bad person may say something rude in a time of anger, and that wouldn't be their proudest moment. But we are all human. We all make mistakes. And that doesn't make them bad, but they do regret it. An evil person does several bad things, they begin to pile up into a pile of lies and hatred, and they don't regret what they've done. They just keep doing it. Even though they know it is wrong." Kohl looked from me to Aria, an unreadable, yet strong, expression on his face.

Kohl continued, "Maria switched sides because she knew what she was doing was bad. She stopped killing the innocent at your will. Maria stopped herself before she became a heartless person. Before she became evil. But, you, you just kept going and going and going. Everything you have ever done has impacted someone in some way. You never thought about that part of it, did you? And, if you did, it is quite clear you never paid enough attention to it. You murder innocent men and women for something you cannot forgive. Something that would be so easy to forgive. You force people to work at your will and, if they don't meet your expectations, they are executed. That is a truly terrible thing to do. You, the Queen of Avion, a whole continent, are evil. Truly evil."

The Queen looked bewildered at Kohl's statement. It even left me speechless. The roaring of the battle rang out from the gates of the garden. The clashing of steel on steel and the cries of wounded men and women were very prominent. I couldn't focus. I didn't even know I was speaking as I heard the loud words that seemed to make the garden hold its breath.

"Step down, Aria. Or face the consequences!"

## 33

Aria sneered at me as she barked a command at her faithful wolves. They seemed reluctant but Manjin and Lupu stood attentive at her side, standing in a position to attack.

"What do you plan to do?" she asks, commanding the dogs to start to circle us intently.

As they draw in closer, Lupu nips at Kohl's leg, where he then kicks him out of the way. Lupu snarls in response but doesn't try it again.

The Queen starts to walk closer as I say, "Two wrongs don't make a right. But, in this case, I'd beg to differ."

Before I know what is even happening, the Queen yells out, "Arveck!" I wasn't ready as Manjin and Lupu started to attack us. They seemed sorrowful about it. I would make sure they were not killed in the fight. As firmly but, as softly as possible, push Manjin off of my chest, and onto the ground. As much as I fear I hurt him, his whimper only lasted but a second before he and Lupu switched spots. I felt Lupu's teeth sink into my ankle and I tried not to howl in pain. Kicking off Lupu's attack, I knew there had to be something up. The teeth marks were barely bleeding. The pups had to have been going easy on us.

"Kohl!" I shout over the clash of outside swords. "Get Lupu and Manjin inside! I can handle the rest."

He nods in approval and leads the wolves inside through lots of tricking. As soon as they are out of the line of sight of Aria, the wolves relax, wagging their tails and licking their savior's face. Something tells me Aria wasn't the nicest to them.

"Now that your wolves are gone, who are you going to hide behind?" I ask as I draw closer. I have two heavy daggers in each hand, my fingers nimbly wrapping around the ornate ebony hilts. "I won't let my training go to waste," I assure her. I draw in closer, springing into action.

She wears a face of fear as she watches me close in and, unsure of what to do, she tumbles out of the way. Stumbling to her feet, she starts to run, tripping occasionally over stones or potholes. I let her get in front of me. I let her think she would win. I watched my footing as I scaled a tree to get a better look at my target. Hopping agilely from one tree branch to another, I followed her silently in the trees. She stopped for a breath after we were long out of the sprawling garden. I was unsure of where we were, actually. It was like a ring of trees and in the middle was the Queen, and the light seemed to funnel light upon her. She looked frantically around her, her eyes and head darting around her surroundings.

I wasn't going to kill her. Not yet. Not unless I had to. I jumped down from the trees. I heard a yelp and then a little snap as I landed on top of her.

Her heart was beating rapidly as I spoke to her, "You can have another chance," I whisper to her, my dagger pressed to her throat so she would attempt an escape. "But not here. Never here. If you move, if you leave, get a ship to a different continent, get out of here, you can live. Do you hear me?" She doesn't speak, and I press the dagger into her throat harder. She gulps before I ask the question again. She gulps before letting out a dry laugh.

"Look what you've done, Maria. You have left a continent of people without a government. Without a queen. What do you plan to do now?"

"I don't know," I admit.

"Let me go. Let me remain as your Queen. I will let you and Kohl go. Punishment free. The choice is yours."

For a moment, I am tempted to take her deal and end the madness that has begun. I push those thoughts out of my head.

"No," I say, pushing the dagger a little bit harder. Blood starts to trickle from her neck. It's barely any, but it is still there, running like a drippy faucet.

She remains silent.

I need Kohl. I need to know what to do.

I call his name, once, twice, three times before he appears through the bush.

"Are you okay?" he says running to my side.

"What do I do?" I say, begging him for an answer. "Do we kill her? Or do we let her go? Not here, of course. We could send her off on a boat. If she never returns, our ordeal will be over,'"' I say. A tear started to run down my eye. Only one.

He looks down at the half-dead woman before us. My dagger lay on the ground next to her, and Aria had her hand pressed over her throat.

He looked into my eyes and I could see what his answer was. He knows I get the message, but he says it aloud anyway.

"You should let her go."

The Queen's eyes grew large in size as Kohl spoke in a strong tone, "This is your only chance. We will send you off on a boat to Mariden. If you ever come back, you will be shot on sight, do you hear me?"

She nods, and whispers, "I knew you'd make the right choice."

I try to believe those words. I don't know if I can.

## 34

The next few hours were chaos. While Kohl and Jackie arranged, a boat for the Queen, I helped clean up the sight of the battle. Bodies of foes and friends lay strewn across the grass, their bodies baking in the heat. I gave everyone that I could a proper burial, but some of the bodies didn't have enough left to bury them.

After the bodies were all cleaned up, we walked the Queen to the boat, the remains of my army, about fifty people, trailed behind, battered and bloody but still holding their weapons high. We walk for a while, back through the town where the castle resides until we reach Baylen Harbor. There was a group of townspeople who followed our trail, some gawking, some silent but with wonder on their faces. I walk onto the dark wooden boat and bring her to the cabin she will be in for the long two-month journey.

"You will be shackled to the leg of your bed. We can't risk you trying to overthrow the crew. You will have full roam of the cabin," I say to her, using my hands to move around the room. It wasn't much. A single bed with a thin sheet, an armchair, and a closet. As we left the boat, she didn't say anything. Not a thank you, a farewell, or even a smile. It wasn't like I cared, anyway. If I didn't see the look in Kohl's eyes when he realized there was an alternate option, we wouldn't even be here right now.

Kohl, Jackie, and I, along with a large group of people, stood on the peer and watched as the giant boat pulled away from the harbor. There was a lot of yelling; some cheers of joy, some boos, but the most prominent sound over all of the racket was the sound of my name.

"Maria, Maria, Maria!" The voices of hundreds of people filled my ears followed by the saying, "The Queen has been removed from the land! The gods have answered our prayers!"

I smiled, any thoughts of regret leaving my mind in an instant. Kohl smiled, his grin so wide it could be seen from even the furthest distance.

"We did it," he whispered into my ear and held me in a tight hug.

"Yes," I said softly. "Yes, we did."

Pulling away from his grasp, I calmed the riled people as I spoke, "Everyone, please, settle down!" The sound of the remaining voices slowly dwindled out and then I began once more. Putting together a speech in my head as fast as I could, I spoke, the words flowing out with an easy grace,

"This kingdom has been ruled by a once lovely ruler, or so we thought. For as long as we and our ancestors can remember, the royal family has always been corrupt. They forced young men and women to work for them at their will and, if they were deemed not good enough, they were to be tossed out with the trash. We have been silent for far too long. It was time to fight back!"

Mostly cheers erupted from the crowd of people, with only the occasional boo. Even some members of the Queen'" Council cheered aloud.

"What will happen to you, Miss Maria?" one curious little girl shouted to me once the chaos had quieted.

"That is a great question, that I, quite frankly, don't have the answer to. But, whatever it is, even if it is something horrible or something great, I will be ready to face it." I smiled at the little girl with the big, brown doe-like eyes and the blonde braids.

"You should be our new queen!" she squealed and giggled at the idea.

Her mom hugged her close and said, "I apologize for her, she doesn't quite understand."

"No, no, it's quite all right," I assure her, but my mind is spinning with that thought. It was silly, and certainly not possible, and it came from a little girl, but the thought was swarming in my head the whole time that I was answering the questions of dozens of curious people.

That was until one of the members of the Queen's Council asked me the question, "Maria, I am sure you remember me, but what do you plan on doing after this? "

I, of course, remembered him. He was always my favorite out of all the members; tall and broad with a kind face, and those crinkles you get in your eye when you smile.

"I don't really know," I admit. "I didn't think about it. I may just go on with my life. Try to pretend like it never happened."

He chuckled, slicking back his graying hair, as he said, "Well, I think that this young girl's idea was quite brilliant, wouldn't you agree?" he said, now talking more so to the gathering of people and not me. There were cheers and more yelling, but ,to my surprise, not one boo.

"I, Sir Roriand, the head of the Queen's Council, am formally asking you if you'd be interested in taking on the task of becoming our new queen?"

# 35

My throat felt as if it was going to swell, and I found myself unable to talk for a moment.

"It by no means would be a quick process; we would have to gather a lot of information, and at least three other council members would have to vote for you to be placed as the queen. But, I think that you are a strong, capable young woman and you would be a perfect fit for our kingdom."

The roaring, shouting and cheers of everyone around me drowned out all of the words I was trying to say aloud. I turned to Kohl, where his smile had grown even larger than it was before.

"I think," he started in, pulling me closer to him, "You would be the perfect fit." I smile, pulling him into a hug. I still need a moment to think. I am unsure of a lot of things, but one wrong word and I could have myself in a mess. "You should do it," Kohl assured me.

Jackie appeared from behind us, wrapping me in a hug, before repeating Kohl's words, "You would be perfect," she beams.

Once I turn to face the sea of people before me, everyone quiets, even the sound of the ocean lapping against the beach seems to soften as if it's holding its breath in anticipation.

"I will do it, on one condition; Kohl gets to stay. Maybe act as a King of sorts," I smile, looking at him as his face turned red.

The people before us laughed, giggled and agreed with me at the statement, before Sir Roriand shouted over them, "It is official! Why don't we do the vote now, everyone back up! Council members step forward!" he commanded.

Slowly, everyone started to back up as four neatly dressed people walked to stand neatly lined up in front of me and Kohl.

Sir Roriand joined them until there were five finely dressed people ready, two women and three men.

"I will go first," Sir Roriand announced, stepping to face the rest of the council members. "From me, it is a yes. I think Maria would be a fine, beautiful queen for our land." He gave a little bow. One vote. Two more. My heart was racing as a woman with bright ginger hair who was dressed in an emerald green dress stepped forward. I barely remembered her, but her face was cold, yet expressionless. She turned and was talking to me rather than the council.

"For me, It is a no."

My heart sank, but she continued talking,

"She is only a girl. Twenty-six is no age for a ruler. I am sure that she could make a fierce leader, but I feel that she would be better off if she stayed out of politics." She turned up her nose and headed back into the line.

The next person, another woman with shiny blonde hair, gave me a yes, stating that a young woman will be able to rule a longer, more victorious reign than an older person could.

My heart was racing. Two yesses, two noes. The last person would determine my fate. He was a wise-looking soul, with a gray mustache and heavily hooded, blue eyes.

I trembled as he spoke but listened to every. single. word.

"Well, I may not agree with Maria's actions, but I won't lie to you all. She has given us a wonderful opportunity that we should not pass up. I do remember her from the time she served in the castle; she was always kind to all, even the servants, and I think that Maria would make a wise leader. My vote is a yes."

Cheers rang out through the crowd once more, and the old man, I think his name was David, looked at me and gave a wink.

"The coronation will be next Saturday at sundown for all who wish to attend!" announced Sir Roriand.

I smiled, hugging Kohl as tightly as I could.

"I think we will do great things," I said softly, looking up at him.

"I think that you are right," he agreed.

## 36

I stood in my new bedroom, the Queen's bedroom, which was very different from the others. Beautiful sprawling ceilings, a large, soft bed, even my own equally as large bathroom. It was more than enough for one person.

I grabbed my coronation outfit. It was a lithe, white dress complete with little lace flowers. I was never a fan of dresses, but this one was special.

"Today is the day," Jackie said excitedly.

I smiled at her, my stomach threatening to spew unwanted things onto my white dress if I spoke. As she laced up the back of the dress, my mind wandered through the events that were going to happen today. First, would be the coronation itself. After that, there would be a little celebration, maybe some cake and dancing. After that, I wasn't sure. All I knew was that I was excited. Once Jackie had finished curling my hair and doing my makeup, I was ready. I walked over to the full-length mirror that was placed on the ornate marble floors. I gasped when I saw my reflection. I had never seen myself look so put together before, with my dark hair placed in a delicate updo and my face with a very natural makeup look.

"Do you like it?" Jackie asked as she walked up behind me and placed a hand on my shoulder.

"I love it," I say, trying to hold back my smile.

"Do a spin," she asked.

Placing my arms out to my sides and trying not to fall in the white heels that were on my feet, I spun in a circle. The dress fluttered around me, making the moment even more whimsical. Once I stopped, I looked at myself in the mirror once more. I was happy, there was no denying that. But, in a way, it felt wrong. I felt as if I shouldn't be the one standing in this gown. I was starting to regret my agreement to become the queen. It was a great deal of power and I would do good with it.

I couldn't back out now, so, when Jackie looked at me and said, "It's time to go show them what you can do," I didn't resist. Making my strides as long as I could and depicting myself as confident as possible, I strode through the throne room into the garden. It was beautiful, with tables with platters of food and drinks, and soft music playing, floating through the air. When I saw Kohl waiting by the spot in the trees where the ceremony would take place, I had to resist the urge to run to him. Walking as slowly as possible, I greeted him with a simple hello.

He was dressed more fancily than usual, in a black suit and a silver tie, chatting expectantly with a man I haven't seen before.

"You look stunning," he said, switching his attention over to me and away from the man he was talking with.

"Same goes for you," I say with a giggle, "I have never seen you in anything other than sweatpants."

He fakes a scowl at me but then laughs along with the joke.

"This is my father," he says with a kind smile. "Dad, this is Maria."

"It's nice to meet you, Queen Maria. I think that you will do wonderfully, and I do apologize for any inconveniences I may have caused you."

I return the smile that he offered and said,"No, you are quite all right, you weren't an inconvenience at all."

He gives a half-hearted chuckle and says, "It was nice to meet you, Queen Maria."

"You too, sir."

"Please, call me Levi."

"Noted," I say with a smile. He returns that smile and Kohl turns over to me.

"Are you ready?" Kohl asks me.

"If I am being completely honest with you, no, I'm not. I feel as if my world is spinning in a thousand directions and I don't know which one to follow. I don't think I'm cut out for this, but it is too late to back out now. I will be the best queen I can be."

He gives me a sorrowful smile before he says, "I think you are perfect for the job. You are smart, capable, and a kind person to everyone."

I look at him, a grin displayed on my face and my heart beating loud in my chest, before I say to him, "I could always use a king, you know."

It took him a minute to fully understand what I said, but, when he does, his face turns a bright shade of beet red. However, that only lasted but a second, and he quickly replies, "And I could use a queen."

It was my turn to blush and, as he pulled me in, I wasn't ready for his lips to be pressed against mine. I didn't really mind it, they were soft and gentle. He pulled away after a second. It was the best second of my life, even though it was quick.

I beamed at him, wrapping my arms around him as the crowd of people coming to watch the ceremony let out cheers and awes.

Sir Roriand was quick on the scene as he said with a sort of smirk, "I had a feeling this was going to happen. Therefore, I have brought the king's crown as well."

The gathering of people made sounds of happiness, as the ceremony began.

"Maria. You are a headstrong, kindhearted, lovely woman. You are going to be the best leader that our kingdom has seen in a long, long time. Do you have any words for your people?"

I nod before saying as loudly as I could, "We have lived in fear of becoming older for as long as we can remember. We will no longer face that fear! The first law that I will put into action will remove the Sorting Act the previous queen put in place!"

I could see the pleasure and joy on everyone's faces, but, out of respect, all they did was clap.

"Thank you, Maria. We all appreciate that. Now, Kohl. You are a capable young man, who will be a perfect fit for the king of our land, and I truly think that you and Maria will make astonishing leaders. Anything you would like to address?"

Kohl looks around at the gathering of people and tries to smile as he says, "The choice to send the Queen away was a difficult one, and we certainly did not take the choice lightly. I just want to make it known that we will have everyone's best interest at heart, and we did not plan on this outcome. We thought that we would be tried for murder, but I am glad that most of us can see eye to eye. Thank you." Kohl finishes his statement with a low bow, and the crowd gave a strong clap.

"That was a bold statement, and I am glad to know that you will both consider thoughts from the council. Now, time for the crowning. Maria, darling, please step forward," Sir Roriand smiled affably at me.

I tried not to shake as I bowed my head, and Sir Roriand placed an intricately woven silver circlet on my head. The pieces of silver were woven in a way where they met in the middle, housing a single round, shiny sapphire. I smiled as the crowd shook with applause and then Sir Roriand moved on to Kohl, where he also bowed his head, allowing Sir Roriand to place a circular crown upon his head. Kohl's was slightly more simple than mine but still astonishing. It was also made of silver, with five points going around the crown, each topped with a sapphire gemstone.

"I now pronounce you King and Queen of Avion!"

The claps of many people rang out throughout the crowd, and I embraced Kohl once more.

"We did it," Kohl said with a smile.

"We did, didn't we?" I reply in a soft, yet encouraging tone.

"Are you ready to start a new life?" he asks with a grin.

"I think I am," I said and, though my smile was true as I gazed back out at the crowd of clapping people, some part of me felt like it was only just the beginning.